She Thre
Straig

D0831543

It disintegrated with a pleasingly loud smash.

Jude jerked open the door and glared at her. "Planting a garden? Aren't you a few months early?"

"I know something I'd like to plant," she returned, and her eyes measured him from head to toe. She bent to pick up the shards of pottery.

Jude bent to help her and their heads collided. He caught her shoulders to keep her from pitching over backward. His eyes searched hers, and they both rose to their feet.

His darkening eyes moved slowly down to her mouth as hers went to his. For a long, long time she'd wondered how it would feel if he kissed her. Part of her had feared it, but another part was hungry for it.

He bent his head toward her. . . .

DIANA PALMER

is a prolific romance writer who got her start as a newspaper reporter. Accustomed to the daily deadlines of a journalist, she has no problem with writer's block. In fact, she averages a book every two months. Mother of a young son, Diana met and married her husband within a week: "It was just like something from one of my books."

Dear Reader:

SILHOUETTE DESIRE is an exciting new line of contemporary romances from Silhouette Books. During the past year, many Silhouette readers have written in telling us what other types of stories they'd like to read from Silhouette, and we've kept these comments and suggestions in mind in developing SILHOUETTE DESIRE.

DESIREs feature all of the elements you like to see in a romance, plus a more sensual, provocative story. So if you want to experience all the excitement, passion and joy of falling in love, then SILHOUETTE DESIRE is for you.

Karen Solem
Editor-in-Chief
Silhouette Books

DIANA PALMER
The Rawhide Man

Silhouette Desire
Published by Silhouette Books New York
America's Publisher of Contemporary Romance

SILHOUETTE BOOKS, a Division of Simon & Schuster, Inc.
1230 Avenue of the Americas, New York, N.Y. 10020

Distributed by Pocket Books

ISBN: 0-671-49599-2

First Silhouette Books printing September, 1984

10 9 8 7 6 5 4 3 2 1

America's Publisher of Contemporary Romance

Printed in the U.S.A.

Books by Diana Palmer

Silhouette Romance

Darling Enemy #254
Roomful of Roses #301
Heart of Ice #314

Silhouette Special Edition

Heather's Song #33

Silhouette Desire

The Cowboy and the Lady #12
September Morning #26
Friends and Lovers #50
Fire and Ice #80
Snow Kisses #102
Diamond Girl #110
The Rawhide Man #157

To Doris, Kay, Kathleen, June, Mary, Cindy, Sharalee and all those lovely San Antonio ladies

The Rawhide Man

1

Thunder was crashing wildly outside the elegant middle Georgia house, but the poised young woman standing in the parlor was too numb to be frightened of it. The ordeal of the past two days had stripped her nerves of all feeling.

Elizabeth Meriam White was twenty-two and felt fifty. Her mother's lingering illness had been torment enough, but she hadn't expected the loss to be so traumatic. Wishing only the peace of oblivion for her beloved parent, she hadn't realized how empty her own life was going to become. Now she had no one. Her stepsister had left that morning for Paris in a whirl of expensive perfume and chiffon, with her share of their mother's estate firmly in hand. They'd never been close, but Bess had hoped for something more after the ordeal. She should have known better. Crystal had never once offered to help nurse her dying stepmother. After all, she'd told Bess carelessly, there was plenty of money to hire someone to do that.

Plenty of money. Bess could have cried. Yes, there had been, until Bess's father died and her mother remarried to Jonathan Smythe and turned her father's business interests over to him. Carla had never bothered with finance, except to make sure that the Rawhide Man couldn't get his hands on that precious block of shares in the Texas oil corporation his father and Bess's had pioneered together.

Bess shivered at the thought of Jude Langston. She'd always thought of him as rawhide through and through, because he was like that—lean and tough and very nearly invulnerable. He hadn't been at the funeral, but Bess had seen her mother's will and she knew he'd be along. Even in death, Carla's obsession with besting Jude went on.

With a long sigh, Bess walked to the window and watched the rain beating down outside on the bleak, barren trees, whose autumn leaves had only just disappeared as cold December hovered overhead.

She leaned her forehead against the cold windowpane and closed her eyes. Oh, Mama, she thought miserably, I never knew what loneliness was until now. I never knew.

It had been a long year. A long two years. Carla had had a progressive kind of bone cancer that hadn't responded to any kind of treatment, not radiation or chemotherapy. And Carla herself had refused any discussion of bone marrow transplants. So her death had been by inches, while Bess had tried to be brave and nurse her and not go to pieces. It hadn't been easy. Her mother had been demanding and perverse and irritable and impatient. But Bess loved her. And she took care of her, up until the final hospital stay. She did it without any help from Crystal, too, because Crystal was having a mad fling with a French count and couldn't be bothered to come home. Except to grab her share of the pitiful amount of money that was left, of course. Bess had reminded her coldly that hospital and doctor bills had drained the family resources. And then Crystal had asked about the oil stock. . . .

Bess rubbed the back of her neck where it felt strained to the limit. She was sick all over with grief and the lack of rest and food. The stock, Crystal had said, might pull Bess out of the hole.

"Even so, you'll have to sell the house, Bess," Crystal had said, oddly sympathetic. "It's mortgaged to the roots of the grass."

"The minute he hears from the attorneys, Jude Langston will come down on my head like judgment," Bess returned, "and you know it."

"That sexy man," Crystal said, nodding dreamily. "My God, what a waste, to look like that and be as hard as he is. He could have women by the barrelful, but all he wants to do is play around with oil and cattle and that baby of his."

"Katy's not a baby anymore," Bess reminded her. "She's almost ten."

"That's right, you go to the ranch every summer, don't you, to those reunions? But you didn't go this summer . . . ," Crystal remarked.

Bess colored delicately and turned away. "I had to take care of mother," she said shortly.

"Yes, I know it was hard. I'd have helped, darling, really I would, but . . ." Her delicate features twisted. "What will you do about the stock?"

"I wish I didn't have it," Bess said levelly. "I don't relish having to face Jude. I only wish mother hadn't tied up the stock the way she did."

"Oh, she hated him, all right," Crystal laughed. "Even when she was able, she'd never go to the reunions, because she knew he'd be there. Why were they such enemies?"

"Because she was a society girl," Bess said bitterly, remembering. "And there's nothing in the world Jude hates more. Katy's mother was one, you know. She broke their engagement while he was in Vietnam and married someone else, even though she was carrying his child. He still takes that hatred out on anyone handy. Mother. Or me. I just wish the battle had died with her."

"I think you'll manage, sweet," Crystal told her, sizing up her stepsister's tall, elegant carriage. Bess wasn't exactly pretty, but she was a lady and she had class, and it stuck out all over her, from her silver blond hair to her soft brown eyes and creamy complexion.

"Against Jude?" Bess smiled sadly. "I watched him back down an armed cowboy once, when I was with Dad at the Langston ranch. I was about fourteen, and one of the hands got mad at Jude for something. He took a couple of drinks and went at Jude with a loaded gun. Jude didn't even flinch. He walked straight into the gun, took it away from the cowboy and beat him to his knees."

"Your eyes flash when you talk about him," Crystal observed, watching Bess. "He excites you, doesn't he?"

"He frightens me," the older girl laughed nervously.

Crystal shook her head slowly. "You're awfully naive for a woman your age. It isn't fear, but you aren't experienced enough to know that, are you?" she asked absently. Then she shrugged and whirled away. "Have to run, pet; Jacques is meeting me at the airport. Let me know how things work out, won't you?"

And that was that. Bess was left alone in the house, and it was getting dark. She had no family, no close friends—there hadn't been the opportunity to make friends, with an invalid mother who needed constant care. So she was alone.

Involuntarily her mind went wandering back to Jude like a puppy that wouldn't mind. He'd be along, all right. As soon as he realized that Bess had control of his precious stock, he'd be at her throat. He hadn't managed to run over Carla, though, and he wasn't going to run over Bess, either. She had the shares and she was keeping them. They were all that stood between her and starvation, and they paid a high dividend.

She let the curtain fall and turned away from the window too quickly to catch the flash of car lights against the glass. The force of the rain muffled the sound of a purring engine coming closer.

Bess went into the bare hall and sat down on the steps, ruffling her disheveled blond hair. She touched her face lightly, mentally comparing it with Crystal's. Her nose was arrow-straight; her mouth had a bee-stung appearance, full and red and soft. Her brown eyes were wide-spaced and appealing. She wasn't beautiful like her stepsister, but she wasn't ugly, at least. Of course, she was very thin and small breasted—not voluptuous like Crystal. But someday she might find a man and get married. And again she thought of Jude and cursed her stubborn, stupid mind. Jude would never marry. For heaven's sake, he'd never even bothered to marry Katy's mother!

Bess stared around her at the opulent home, which had been part of the White estate for over a hundred years, surviving even the Civil War. How sad that it hadn't been able to survive the Smythes, she thought with a surge of humor. Crystal was right, of course. It would have to be sold. Dividends from her stocks would provide enough to support her if she was frugal, but not to maintain the house as well.

With a weary groan she got to her feet. She might as well get busy and clean out some drawers or something. It would have been a blessing if she'd had a job to go to, but she'd been trained for nothing except managing this monstrous house. And soon she wouldn't have even that. She laughed almost hysterically at the thought. She'd have to get a job.

The sudden clang of the doorbell made her jump. She hadn't expected visitors in this wild rain.

She glanced at her hair in the mirror: it looked as if it had been caught in a windmill, but there was no time to fix it, and she wasn't wearing makeup at all. She looked pale and plain and sickly. She hoped this wasn't going to be another bill collector; she had enough trouble already, and the phone calls and demands for payment were growing hourly since the news of her mother's death had been made public. When it rained it poured, she thought desperately.

A wild shudder went through her when she opened the door. The man outside was the image of every woman's secret dream. Tall, broad shouldered and long legged, dressed in an expensive gray pinstriped suit with matching Stetson and boots, he looked like something out of a smart men's magazine. But his face, deeply tanned, was as inscrutable as a stone carving. His mouth was rigid, as firm as his jaw. His eyes were deeply set under thick black lashes and they were a glittering pale green. His scowling eyebrows were the same jet black as the hair she glimpsed under his hat. And the whole portrait was so formidable that she instinctively stepped back.

"You've been expecting me, I imagine," Jude Langston said curtly, just a trace of a Texas accent in his deep, measured voice.

"Oh, yes, along with flood, earthquake and volcanic eruptions," she agreed, using the protective guise of humor that had always saved her nerves when she had to deal with him. "I won't even bother asking why you're here. Obviously, you've seen the will."

He moved forward, and she knew him too well to stand her ground. He closed the door roughly behind him, and rain dripped from the wide brim of the gray hat that shadowed part of his face.

"Where can we talk?"

She turned, remembering that she was still Miss White of Oakgrove, and led him into the shabby parlor.

"Still the society girl, I see," he taunted, dropping down onto the sofa. "Do I get coffee, Miss White, or aren't the servants working today?"

She blanched, but her chin lifted and her brown eyes accused. "My mother died two days ago," she said pointedly, "so could you save your sarcasm for a special occasion? Yes, there's coffee; and no, there aren't any servants. There haven't been for a number of years. Or don't you know yet that the only thing standing between me and imminent starvation is that block of oil shares you're so hot to get your hands on?"

He looked as if she'd actually surprised him, but she turned away. "I'll get the coffee," she said curtly.

While she was gone, she cooled down her hot temper. It wouldn't do her any good with Jude; the only chance she had was to keep her head and not go for his throat. By the time she carried the worn silver service into the living room, he'd discarded his topcoat and hat and was wandering around the room, glancing distastefully at the portrait of Carla and Bess above the mantel.

He turned and watched her set the heavy service on the coffee table without offering to help. That was like him, the original chauvinist who had no time for women.

"Thank you," she said elegantly, "for your kind assistance."

"Is the damned thing heavy?" he asked carelessly.

She almost laughed. The situation was unbelievable. She sat down and poured out the coffee, handing him his black without realizing what that little slip gave away.

"Should I be flattered that you remember how I take my coffee?" he asked, leaning back to study her insolently, running his eyes over every curve outlined by the simple gray jersey dress she was wearing.

"Don't put on your cowboy drawl for me, mister," she replied quietly, lifting her cup to her lips. "I know you."

"You think you do," he agreed, his green eyes narrowing.

"How's Katy?" she asked.

He shrugged. "Growing up fast." His gaze focused on her. "She asked about you when the family got together this summer."

"I'm sorry I missed it," she said. "I couldn't leave Mother."

He flexed his broad shoulders and leaned forward. The action stretched the fabric of his pants over his powerful thighs and Bess had to look away.

"That's enough small talk," he said suddenly, piercing her eyes with his. "You're coming back to San Antonio with me."

She hardly had time to catch her breath. "I'm what?"

"You heard me." He set down his cup. "The only way I can control that stock is by marrying you. So that's how we'll do it."

Her body jerked as if he'd hit her, and she stared at him uncomprehendingly. She might have thought of this before—it was so like Jude to take the direct approach.

"No," she said shortly.

"Yes," he replied. "I've waited years to get my hands on those shares, and I'm having them. If you come along with the deal, I'll just have to make the best of it."

She went red in the face and sat up straight. "What makes you think you're any prize?" she asked in her coldest tone. "You're cold and hard and you don't care about anybody in the world except Katy!"

"That's absolutely gospel," he agreed, staring at her unblinkingly. "But you'll go to the altar with me if I have to tie you up and gag you, except for the part where you say, 'I do.'"

"I do not," she corrected. "You can't force me to marry you."

"Think not?" He stood up, his green eyes glittering with cold humor, his face confident and frighteningly hard.

He left the room, and Bess stood up, staring helplessly around. What in the world was he doing!

Minutes later he was back, with her coat in one hand and her purse dangling from his fingers. He slung them at her. "I've undone the fuse box. You can call a real estate agent from San Antonio and put the house on the auction block. Any little things you want can be shipped out. Now put on that coat."

She couldn't believe this was happening. It must be a hallucination brought on by the strain, she told herself. But a minute later, always impatient, he was stuffing her into the coat. He jerked the hood up and thrust the purse into her hands.

"I won't go!" she cried out.

"Like hell you won't go." He bent and swung her up into his arms like a sack of feathers and carried her out into the rain.

2

~oooooooooo~

This isn't happening, Bess told herself an hour later as she sat beside Jude in the cockpit of his big Cessna. It simply isn't happening!

But the sound of the engine was very real, and so was Jude's set, humorless face as he concentrated on flying the plane.

Characteristically, he wasn't trusting his life to another pilot. He liked having total control—in everything. That was why he was flying himself and that was why he wanted the block of shares that Bess now owned. It was also, Bess suspected, why no woman had ever managed to get him to the altar in a conventional way. Falling in love would be giving a measure of control to someone else too.

She leaned back in the seat, staring blankly at the

clouds ahead, and wondered how she was going to get herself out of this predicament. Surely some other way could be found to give him the stock, if he reimbursed her. She brightened. Until she remembered the exact wording of the will. She muttered under her breath. Carla had taken care of that angle, too. The only way Jude could possibly get the stock was to marry Bess. And that, Carla had smugly thought, he'd never do. He disliked Bess. Everyone knew it, too. They fought like cats and dogs, and people moved out of the way at Langston family get-togethers when they were both present.

The reunion two summers ago was the reason Bess had stayed away from the most recent gathering. She and Jude had gotten into a horrible fight about Katy. She could still blush at the language he'd used; the fact that there had been bystanders present hadn't slowed him down one iota.

Katy had told Bess about a fight she'd been in at school, stating proudly that she'd done just like Daddy, she'd pounded the hell out of a boy twice her size, and wasn't that super? "Super" had been Katy's latest word; it described everything from her dog, Pal, to the calf Jude had given her to raise for 4-H.

Bess hadn't thought it was super now that Katy was eight. She'd thought it was terrible, and she'd told Jude so later as they were sitting together having dinner with some of the other family members at a restaurant on the Paseo del Rio. Traditionally, they always concluded the annual picnic and rodeo at the restaurant, which Jude would book for an arm and a leg and the family would fill.

"What's wrong with Katy sticking up for herself?" he'd demanded. "The damned boy hit her first."

"She's a girl," Bess had burst out, exasperated with him. "For heaven's sake, she already dresses and talks like a boy. What are you trying to do to her?"

"Teach her to stand up for herself," he'd replied coolly, and had gone back to sipping his whiskey, raising his hand as another male member of the family entered the restaurant.

"Teaching her to be a freak," Bess had said under her breath.

That had set him off. She could still see him rising, as slowly as a rattlesnake coiling, his eyes glittering and dangerous, his face taut.

"Katy is my daughter," he'd said with a cold smile. "I decide what's good or bad for her, and I don't need help from some dainty little society lady who couldn't fight her way out of an eclair! Who the hell do you think you are to tell me how to raise my daughter? What qualifies you to be anybody's mother?" His voice was raised just enough to carry to the other tables, and there was a sudden hush, broken only by the sound of the river and the muffled voices of strolling passersby on the river walk. Bess had wanted to cringe.

"People are staring," Bess had said under her breath.

"Well, my God, let them stare!" he'd boomed, scowling down at her. "If you're so free with your damned advice on child raising, let's tell everybody. Go ahead, Miss White, do advise me on the behavior of my child!"

Her face was white with embarrassment and humiliation, but she held her head up and stared back at him. "I don't think I need to repeat it," she said very calmly.

It made him even angrier that he couldn't make her lose her composure entirely. That was when he'd started cursing. "You damned little prig," he'd tacked on at the end, and by that time her face was as red as it had been white earlier. "Why don't you get married and have kids of your own? Can't you find a man good enough?" He'd laughed coldly and looked over her body with contempt. "Or can't you find a man?"

And he'd turned and walked away, leaving her sitting there with tears stinging her eyes. The family had lost interest then and gone on to other topics. Bess had gone back to her hotel and packed. It was the last time she'd had any contact with Jude, until now.

"So quiet, Miss White," he taunted, jerking her out of her reveries. "So ladylike. You didn't even kick and scream. Is that kind of behavior too human for you?"

She lifted her chin, her perfect composure intact, and looked at him. "Look who's talking about being human," she said with a cool smile.

One of his thick eyebrows jerked. "But, then, I never claimed to be, did I?"

She averted her eyes. "If I'd had any doubts about it, you'd have quelled them two summers ago."

He made a sound deep in his throat. "You ran," he recalled curtly. "Somehow, I didn't expect that. You've never run from me before."

The wording was unusual and it made her curious, but she wasn't in the mood to start trying to unravel Jude again.

"I didn't run," she replied, telling the lie very calmly. "I simply didn't see any reason to stay an extra day and give you any more free shots at me."

He glanced at her. "I meant what I said about Katy," he said darkly. "I don't want her made into a miniature debutante, is that clear? You lay one hand on her wardrobe and you'll wish you hadn't."

There was no arguing with him when he was in that mood; she knew the look from memory. She turned her face away. "Don't worry, I won't be around long enough to do any damage."

"You'll be around. Now shut up," he added, glaring her way. "I don't like conversation when I'm flying this thing. You wouldn't want to crash, would you?"

"The airplane wouldn't dare," she muttered angrily, glancing at him. "Like most everything else around you, it's too intimidated to take the chance!"

Surprisingly, he laughed. But it was brief, and

then his face was the familiar hard one she was accustomed to.

They landed at the San Antonio airport late that night, and Bess was exhausted. She barely noticed her surroundings until they were heading toward the exit and she got a good look at the walls. They were hung with paintings, all for sale, all exquisite, and most all of Western subject matter.

"Oh, how beautiful!" she exclaimed over one, which showed a ranch house and a windmill overlooking a vast expanse of desert land. It looked like West Texas might have looked a hundred years ago, and she was instantly in love with it.

"Come on, for God's sake," Jude muttered, dragging her away with a steely hand on her arm. The touch went through her like fire.

"Could you stop grumbling for one minute?" she asked him, glaring up, and it was a long way despite her two-inch heels and her five feet, seven inches of height. "And glaring and scowling . . ."

He lifted an eyebrow and looked down his nose at her. "Why don't you stop criticizing everybody around you and take a look at yourself, society girl?" he taunted. "What makes you think you're perfect?"

She knew she wasn't, but it hurt, coming from him. "I won't marry you," she said with controlled ferocity. "Not if you kill me first."

"If I killed you first, there wouldn't be much point in marrying you," he said conversationally. He pulled her along with him. "And you might as well stop arguing. You're going to marry me and that's the end of it."

They stepped out into the nippy air and she tugged her coat closer. It wasn't raining here, but it was cold all the same. The palm trees looked chilly, and the mesquite and oak trees they drove past in Jude's black Mercedes had no leaves on them. They looked as stark as the pecan trees back home.

Pecans reminded her of food, which reminded her that she hadn't had anything to eat since breakfast, and then she remembered what he'd said about turning off the power.

"My gosh, you idiot!" she burst out, turning in the seat. "You cut off the power to the refrigerator!"

He glanced at her. "Don't start name-calling. I've got an edge on you in that department. So what if it spoils? You won't be there to eat it."

"It will smell up the whole house!"

"I'll take care of it," he said calmly. "You can give me the name of a realtor."

"You can't order me to sell Oakgrove!" she burst out irrationally, though earlier she'd made up her mind to do just that. "It's been in my family for over a hundred years!"

"You'll sell it if I say so," he returned, giving her a hard glare. "Shades of Scarlett O'Hara. It's just a piece of land and an old house."

She thought back to all the family picnics, the rides through the woods, the beautiful springs and summers and the loving care that each generation had lavished on the estate. Suddenly it was clear to her that she wouldn't sell it, after all. "No," she said. "It's a legacy. If land is so unimportant, why do you hold on to Big Mesquite?"

"That's different," he said. "It's mine."

"Oakgrove is mine."

"God, you're stubborn," he growled, glaring across the passenger seat at her. "What do you want the place for?"

"It's my home," she told him. "When you come to your senses, I'm going back there to live." And I'll figure out some way to maintain it, she added to herself.

He turned his attention back to the road. "I need those damned shares. Your mother," he added curtly, "has very nearly cost me the corporation I've worked all my life to build up. By denying me the shares that were rightfully mine, she's tied me up in a proxy fight that I've almost lost."

"A proxy fight?" she asked dully.

"I have an enemy on my board of directors," he said shortly, as if it irritated him to have to tell her even that much. "He's shrewd and cunning, and he can sway votes. We're almost even right now. I've got to have that block of shares you own or I'll lose control of the corporation."

"Can't you find some other way to get them?" she asked bitterly.

He sighed. "I've got my attorneys working on it right now, going over your mother's will with a fine-tooth comb. But they aren't optimistic, and neither am I. She's made sure that I can't buy those shares from you. Under the terms of the will, you can't give them to me, either. It looks as if the only way I can control them is to marry you." He glanced sideways, his eyes hot and angry. "It would almost be worth losing the corporation," he muttered, "to send you home."

She drew in a weary breath. "The corporation is your problem. If you can find a way to get the stocks, well and good, but I'm not marrying you. I'd rather starve."

"The feeling is mutual, but neither of us may have any choice."

"I have," she returned.

"Not with me," he replied calmly. "Not a chance in hell. If it takes marriage, you'll marry me."

"I hate you!" she burst out, remembering graphically the humiliation she'd suffered from him. "Give me one good reason why I should even consider being tied to you!"

"Katy," he said simply.

She leaned back against the seat, feeling utterly defeated, and closed her eyes. "You don't want me around Katy; you've said so often enough. I'll corrupt her."

He lit a cigarette as he drove, staring ahead at the streetlit expanse of the sprawling city of San Antonio. "She needs a mother," he said finally. "I've done some thinking about what you said at that reunion. I'm not agreeing that you were right," he added with a glare. "But I'm willing to concede that you weren't totally off base. She's growing up tough. Maybe too tough. A softening influence wouldn't be such a bad idea. And she likes you," he growled, as if that were totally incomprehensible.

"I like her, too," she said quietly, and let him chew on that. "But what are you offering me? You'd be getting control of my shares and a mother for Katy, but what would I get?"

His eyebrows went up. "What do you want? To sleep with me?" He let his eyes wander over her wildly flushed face. "I suppose I could force myself . . ."

"Damn you!" she burst out, hurt by the sarcastic way he'd said it.

He turned his attention back to the road. "Come on, wildcat, tell me what you want."

She shifted restlessly. "Not to be forced into marrying you."

"That's a foregone conclusion." He puffed away on his cigarette. "Tell you what, society girl. If worse comes to worst and we have to go through with it, I'll maintain that antebellum disaster for you, and you and Katy can spend summers there."

She turned her head and studied his unyielding profile. "You would?"

"I would." And he meant it, she knew. When he gave his word, he kept it.

She pursed her lips. "We couldn't just have a quick marriage and a quicker annulment? To satisfy the terms of the will?"

"What would that do to Katy?" he asked suddenly.

She drew in a slow breath and let it out. "Oh."

"Yes, oh. She's so damned excited about having you here, she's half crazy," he said. "I told her," he added with a cold stare, "that you were coming out here so that we could decide whether or not we wanted to get married."

"She'll never believe you want to marry me," she replied tersely.

"Won't she?" A mocking smile curled his lips. "I told her I was nursing a secret passion for you and hoped to win you over."

"You bas—!"

"Uh, uh, uh," he cautioned. "None of those unladylike words, if you please; you'll embarrass me."

"Satan himself couldn't do that," she shot back. "Oh, Jude, let me go home," she moaned. "I can't fight you. I'm too tired."

"Then stop trying. You won't win."

She laughed bitterly. "Don't I know it?" She turned away and looked out the window at the flat horizon as they headed south out of San Antonio. Tears pricked at her eyes as she thought how far away from home she was. From her mother. A sob caught in her throat and tears burst from her eyes as the control she'd maintained so valiantly slipped and broke.

"My God, you don't even cry like a normal woman," he ground out. "Stop that!"

She shook her head and dabbed at the tears. "I loved her," she managed shakily. "It's only been two days, for God's sake, Jude . . . !"

"Well, all the tears in the world won't bring her

back, will they?" he asked irritably. "And in the shape she was in, would you really want to?"

She shifted on the seat. He couldn't understand grief, she supposed, never having felt it. His mother had died when he was an infant, and his father had never been demonstrative. He had been even more unapproachable than Jude, worlds harder. Which was saying a lot, because the Rawhide Man was like steel.

She dashed the tears away and took a deep breath. "I don't want to live with a coldhearted statue like you," she said. "You're . . . you're like rawhide."

"But you'll do it, if it comes to that. You'll do it for Katy's sake." He turned onto the long road that led to the ranch.

"I'll run away!" she said dramatically.

"I'll come after you and bring you back," he said carelessly.

"Jude!" she ground out, exasperated.

"Remember that summer when you were fifteen?" he recalled with a chuckle. "You went out into the brush with Jess Bowman, and I rode all night to find you. You were huddled up in his coat with a twisted ankle, and he was walking down the road trying to flag down a car."

"I remember," she said, shuddering. "You broke his nose."

"I hit when I get mad," he said. "He riled me plenty, leaving you out there alone at night with rattlers crawling and cougars on the loose."

"He couldn't have carried me," she protested.

"I did," he reminded her. "And I wasn't as heavy in those days as I am now."

No, he'd filled out and firmed up and he was devastating. All man. She remembered that brief walk in his hard arms, the strength and power of his frame as he strode along. It was the safest she'd ever felt in her life—and the most afraid.

"That was the summer after Elise died, before I got Katy away from her stepfather. The last summer, too, that you ever spent any length of time at the ranch," he recalled. "That was when you started avoiding me."

She felt her cheeks go hot at the memory. She'd felt something that long-ago night that had haunted her ever since. And because it had frightened her, she'd avoided the ranch whenever possible, except for flying visits to see Katy. And the family reunions, of course, which came frequently during the year. Not that they were really family, but because of the partnership of her father and his, she was always included and expected to take part.

"Why did you stay away?" he asked quietly. "We've had our disagreements over the years, God knows, but I've never hurt you."

That was true enough. She stared down at her hands, folded in her lap. "I don't know," she lied.

He lifted a careless eyebrow. "Were you afraid I'd make a pass?"

She flushed, and he threw back his head and laughed deeply.

"You were fifteen," he reminded her with a chuckle. "And you had even less to draw a man's eye than you do now." His eyes were on her small breasts, and she wanted to dive through the window.

Defensively she folded her arms over her chest and lowered her eyes to the floorboard, so embarrassed that she wanted to cry.

"For God's sake, stop that," he growled. "You'd appeal to some men, I suppose. You just don't appeal to me."

Was that conscience, she wondered numbly? If it was, it didn't console her much.

"I'll get down on my knees and give thanks for that small blessing," she said coldly.

"You're the one with the small blessings, all right," he murmured wickedly.

She half turned in the seat to glare at him, and he chuckled at her fury.

"God, you're something when you get mad," he said with rare mischief. "All dark eyes and wild hair and teeth and claws. It sure as hell beats that so-elegant coolness you wear around you most of the time."

She regained her composure with an effort and stared at him calmly. "My mother raised me to be a lady," she told him.

"You're that," he agreed coldly. "But you'd be a hell of a lot more exciting if she'd raised you to be a woman, instead."

There was no reply to a blatant remark like that, so she turned her attention back to the darkened landscape and ignored him. Which seemed to be exactly what he wanted.

3

~~~~~~~~~~~~~~~~~

Aggie Lopez, Jude's housekeeper, met them in her dressing gown, yawning.

"Is Bess's room ready?" Jude asked curtly.

"Yes, Señor Langston," Aggie said agreeably, giving Bess a brief but thorough appraisal. Then she grinned. "You need some feeding up, señorita. A few weeks of refritos and enchiladas and my good Texas chili will put meat on those bones, I promise you. Come, I will take you up to your room and then I'll bring you some food. The little one has only just gone to sleep. She was so excited . . . !"

"But it's after midnight," Bess exclaimed.

"Go ahead," Jude growled, glaring at her with piercing green eyes, "say something about her bedtime hour. You've managed to disapprove of every other damned thing, why not that as well?"

She glared back at him, her chin lifted. "Children need their rest just like adults do," she threw at him. "And speaking of rest, look at you!"

"What's wrong with me?" he asked pugnaciously.

"Oh, Lord, just give me a full day with no interruptions and I'll be glad to give you an itemized list!"

Aggie was staring at them with her jaw in a slightly drooping posture, her small, plump figure glued to the banister of the long staircase that ran up to the second story.

Jude glanced at Aggie. "Well, what the hell are you gaping at? Are you going to show her upstairs or not?"

"You are . . . really getting married?" the older woman asked, lifting her eyebrows until they almost touched the salt-and-pepper hair that was drawn into a tight bun.

"It's a love match, too," Bess assured her with a tight smile at Jude. "He loves my stocks and I love his daughter."

Jude said something rude under his breath and turned on his heel to stomp off into his study. He slammed the door with hurricane force behind him.

Aggie flinched. "Someday he will break all the windows," she sighed. "Ay, ay, life is so exciting since I came to work here." She eyed Bess. "It is none of my affair, you understand, but you are not the picture of a happy bride."

"I don't want to be a bride," she muttered. "He's trying to make me."

"As I thought," Aggie sighed. She shook her head. "I will not ask why you do not refuse him. Six months I have worked for Mr. Langston. In that time, I have never known him not to get his own way. Have you known him long, señorita?"

"I've known him most of my life," Bess grumbled as she followed the older woman up the staircase.

"Then I do not need to tell you anything about him," Aggie said quietly. She glanced at Bess as she stopped in front of the room where Bess always stayed when she visited the ranch. "He said that you have lost your mother. I am very sorry."

Tears welled up in Bess's eyes and her lower lip trembled precariously. "Yes."

Impulsively, Aggie put an arm around her. "Señorita, grief passes. I, too, lost my mother many years ago. I do not forget the hurt, but time is kind."

Bess nodded jerkily and tried to smile.

"Here, now. Katy insisted on redecorating the room when she heard you were coming." Aggie led Bess into the spacious room, which boasted a new bedspread and matching curtains of cream with beige and blue flowers, a deep blue carpet, and elegant wallpaper. There were fresh flowers, mums, in a vase on the chest of drawers.

"It's beautiful!" Bess burst out.

"Oh, I hoped you'd like it!" came a joyous voice from the connecting door across the room.

Bess's eyes lit up. "Katy!" she exclaimed, and held out her arms.

Katy ran into them, laughing. She was the image of her father—pale green eyes framed by black hair and a stubborn square jaw. She was going to be tall, too. She already came up almost to Bess's shoulder.

"You smell nice," Katy remarked as she drew back to look at the older woman. "Like flowers. You always smell so good, Bess!"

"I'm glad you think so," Bess said with a grin. "How's school?"

Katy made a face. "I hate math and English grammar. But band is great; I play the flute! And I like chorus pretty well, and art class is neat."

"I'd love to hear you play," Bess said. She ruffled the short dark hair. "You're the nicest welcome I've had so far."

"Been at it with Dad again, huh?" Katy murmured with a wicked smile. "I heard," she confessed.

Bess colored delicately. "We, uh, had a slight disagreement."

"They have slight disagreements over the color of the sky," Katy told Aggie without blinking an eye, and she laughed. "Dad likes to give orders and Bess doesn't like to take them."

"Now, Katy . . . ," Bess began.

"I know: 'Now, Katy, mind your own business,'" Katy sighed. She arched her eyebrows. "But you're going to be my mom, so it is kind of my business, isn't it?"

At the sound of the word, Bess's eyes glittered again with unshed tears. She was going to have to stop this!

"Oh, I'm sorry," Katy said quickly, after a speaking glare from Aggie. "I'm very sorry, I forgot!"

"It's all right," Bess said, brushing away the tears. "It's just so fresh, you know. I loved her very much."

"I never knew my mother," Katy said, "but Dad said she was a first-class bit—"

"No!" Aggie burst out, horrified. "You must not say such things!"

Katy's lips pouted. "Dad does."

"Yes, but you shouldn't speak that way of your mother," Bess said gently. "Besides, ladies don't use language like that."

Katy just stared at her blankly. "Huh?"

"You'll have to show me around the ranch tomorrow," Bess said quickly, deciding to let it drop for the time being. "It's more than a year since I visited. I'm sure there are a lot of changes."

That brought the smile back to Katy's young face. "You bet! Unless . . . you wouldn't rather Dad showed you around?" she asked with a calculating look, and Bess knew she was thinking about that dreadful lie Jude had told her.

"He can show me around later," Bess promised the young girl. "Now, how about bed? I'm so sleepy I can hardly stand up."

"Where are your things, señorita, and I will unpack," Aggie volunteered.

"I'm wearing them," Bess said gaily, opening her

coat to disclose the dress underneath. "Jude decided that I could do without clothes, makeup, and all those other frivolous things."

Aggie scowled. "I will lend you one of my gowns," she said. "Men, they never think about these things," she muttered as she went out the door.

Katy was watching her closely. "Why didn't you pack a suitcase?" she asked slowly.

"Because your father picked me up in what I have on and carried me bodily out the door, that's why," she said.

Katy tried to stifle a laugh, but it burst out anyway. "Good night, Bess!" she said, and beat a hasty retreat back to her own room, closing the door quickly. Behind it, there was hysterical laughter.

Bess had forgotten just how big Big Mesquite really was until she walked around the grounds with Katy the next day. The house, which she'd always loved, was very old and very Victorian, with a turret and exquisite gingerbread woodwork. Jude had obviously had it painted not too many months ago, because it was blistering white.

"I remember summers long ago when I used to swing in that front porch swing," Bess recalled dreamily, hanging on to a small mimosa tree in the front yard as she stared toward the house. "And your grandmother would make iced tea and big, thick tomato sandwiches and I'd swing and munch."

"Did you and Dad used to play together?" Katy asked, all eyes.

"No, darling," Bess laughed. "Your father was already a grown man when I was barely in my teens. I hardly ever saw him in those days. He was away in college, and then in Vietnam."

"Oh, yes, I know all about the war," Katy said seriously. "Dad's got an awful—"

"Katy!" Aggie called out the door. "Deanne wants to talk to you on the telephone!"

"Okay, Aggie!" Katy moved away from the tree. "Deanne's my best friend," she explained. "I won't be long."

"Don't hurry on my account," Bess told her. "I'll just ramble around and look at the stock."

"Don't go close to the corral. Dad's got Blanket in there," the young girl cautioned.

"What a name. Does it belong to a bull?"

"No, a horse," Katy laughed. "They call her that because she likes to fall on people—like a blanket."

"I'll watch my step," Bess promised.

Katy ran into the house and Bess wandered quietly around the yard in the same jersey dress she'd worn the day before. She had one of Jude's windbreakers wrapped around herself to keep out the cold, and she hated the pleasure it gave her to wear something of his. She was really going to have to stop feeling that way. If he ever found out how he affected her, it could be a disaster, in more ways than one.

As she was thinking about him, he came out of

the barn with a halter in his hand, heading straight for Blanket.

Bess climbed up on the fence and leaned her arms over the top rail. "Going to bounce around a little?" she asked. "Don't fall off, now."

"No, I'm not going to bounce around," he said curtly. "I'm going to put her on a halter so Bandy can work her."

She watched him approach the horse, talking softly and gently to it in a tone she'd never heard him use except, infrequently, with Katy. He moved close inch by inch, soothing the horse, until he was near enough to ease the halter over the jet black muzzle and lock it in place. He continued to stroke the silky black mane while the horse trembled in the chill air, not from cold but from nervousness.

Bess didn't speak. She didn't dare. Jude would climb all over her if she spooked the horse. But he glanced at her warily when the little bowlegged cowboy named Bandy came out of the barn with a lunging rein to attach to the halter.

Jude said something to the cowboy and then climbed over the fence, perching himself on the top rail near Bess. He was wearing denims and the old battered gray Stetson he used on the rare occasions when he was around the ranch. He looked good in denim. He looked good in anything, that long, muscular body sheer elegance when he moved.

"Don't trust her too far, Bandy," Jude said as he lit a cigarette. He glanced at Bess. "She's a lot like some women. All long legs and nerves."

Her chin lifted. She'd put up her hair to keep it out of her face, and she looked chic and elegant even in his leather jacket.

"Where did you get that?" he asked, indicating the jacket.

"Aggie got it out for me," she said defensively. "You wouldn't let me pack," she reminded him.

"It doesn't do much for you," he remarked derisively.

"It keeps me warm," she returned. "But if you want it back . . ."

"Oh, hell, stop playing Joan of Arc," he growled, his green eyes glittering at her over a wisp of cigarette smoke. "It's an old jacket. I had it when I was in Vietnam."

And probably it brought back memories he'd rather not dredge up, she thought, feeling guilty. She averted her eyes to the cowboy working the young filly on the leading rein in a long, wide circle.

"You didn't hit the floor screaming bloody murder this morning," he remarked. "Does that mean you've stopped fighting the idea of marriage?"

She drew one long, polished fingernail across the top rail of the fence and watched it scar the old wood. "Katy was so excited," she said quietly.

"Yes, I told you that."

Her dark eyes pinned him. "I don't like you very much, Judah Barnett Langston," she said.

He took a long draw from the cigarette and pursed his chiseled lips. "What a disappointment," he said after a minute, and his eyes were mocking. "I thought you might be harboring a secret passion for me."

"Sorry to dash your dreams," she replied. "I'd rather lust after a rattlesnake."

He chuckled softly, and his cold green eyes wandered over her slimness slowly. "You'd have better luck there, all right," he remarked. "Hell, you're too fragile for sex."

She gasped at the unexpectedly intimate remark and felt her face go hot.

His eyebrows lifted at her expression. "Well, my God, I do know what sex is," he said.

"I didn't say a word," she chewed off.

"You were thinking it," he said. He smiled tauntingly. "I didn't find Katy under a cabbage leaf."

Her eyes fell away from his. The discussion was getting far too intimate for her taste. She knew hardly anything about intimacy except for what she'd read. And the last person she wanted to learn that kind of lesson from was Jude Langston. She couldn't picture him being either patient or tender with a woman.

"Is Katy matchmaking?" he asked after a minute. "She deserted you."

"Her friend Deanne called," she murmured.

He scowled. "Deanne is a city kid. Very sophisticated for her age. I don't like Katy associating with her."

"Why, because she wears dresses?" she asked.

"Is Katy going to run the ranch for you when she grows up, bullwhip and all?"

He just stared at her until she dropped her eyes. She'd never been able to outglare him, not ever, and it rankled.

"I wish she'd been a boy sometimes," he said, surprising her. "But that wasn't her fault."

"She's going on ten," she said quietly. "The age of parties and pretty dresses and boys is coming along down the road. It would be sad if she was excluded from all those things because she was too tough to fit in. Wouldn't it?"

He glared at her and threw down his cigarette. "Why don't you mind your own damned business? Go arrange some flowers or something. That's all you're good for!"

He got down off the fence, and tears stung her eyes as she did likewise. She turned on her heel and stomped back off toward the house.

A piercing whistle split the air and she stopped and whirled. "What!" she yelled.

"Go into town and get some clothes. I've opened an account for you at Joske's."

She caught her breath. Things were moving fast. Too fast. "I don't want any, thanks."

"Suit yourself," he said carelessly. "If you want to be married in your slip, it's your business." He turned back to Bandy.

"I'm not going to marry you!" she yelled at him.

"You are if I can't find another way to get those shares!" At that, she almost scooped up a rock and threw it at him. But she knew Jude too well, so she didn't.

By the end of the week, it was sadly apparent that there were no loopholes in Bess's mother's will. Jude came in Friday afternoon looking as if he'd like to tie her to a stake and roast her. Instead, he ordered her into the living room and closed the door behind them.

"There's no way out except marriage," he said without dressing it up. "We can't break the will unless we can prove mental incompetence, and your family attorney assures me that we can't."

"No," Bess sighed, "she was in her right mind up until the very end."

He picked up a book on the table by the window and abruptly slammed it down on the highly polished surface. "Damn it, I don't want marriage!" he cursed, glaring at Bess.

"Well, don't blame me," she shot back. "I didn't drag you off out here and try to force you into it. I'd just as soon forget the whole thing!"

"So would I, but I've got to have those damned shares, and soon. It's no use fighting me, Bess." He rammed his hands in the pockets of his gray slacks. "I'll talk to a minister about the ceremony. We can have it at San Jose, if you like."

"At the mission?" she asked. Her eyes brightened a little. "That sounds nice."

"Then you'll agree to the marriage?" he asked quietly, and she knew he was in deadly earnest.

"I don't seem to have much choice," she replied.

"And you're right—Katy does need a woman's touch. And I need her. I don't have anyone else to love now that Mother's . . ." She broke off, trying desperately to keep the tears from falling. "She was all the family I had in the world."

He turned away, obviously uncomfortable at her show of emotion. "You'd better go to the printer and get some invitations sent out. I'll have my secretary make you a list of people to invite." He glanced at her. "Do you want your stepsister to come?"

"No," she said without thinking.

He laughed shortly. "Somehow, I didn't think you would. But you owe her the courtesy of telling her about the marriage. She is your only living relative."

"I will." Several weeks from now, she added silently.

He studied her. "You don't like Crystal, do you?"

"Neither would you, if she didn't worship the ground you walk on," she said with bitter sarcasm. "Crystal's main ambition in life is to keep Crystal happy and comfortable. But men don't notice that very often."

"No," he agreed, "they're too busy noticing how much woman she is." His eyes went up and down Bess's slender figure. "She puts you in the shade, doesn't she?"

Not for the world would she have let him see how much that hurt. She smiled coolly and turned to leave the room.

"So proud," he chided. "So poised. Does anything ever ruffle you, society girl? I'll bet you'd be that way in bed with a man, all cool discipline and—"

"Stop that," she bit off, glaring at him. "How I'd be is none of your business." She stopped, her eyes uncertain.

He laughed shortly as he read the fear in them. "Don't get your hopes up, Bess. You don't turn me on. It won't be a marriage in that respect."

"Thank God," she muttered, opening the door with her back to him so he couldn't see her hot cheeks.

"I can't imagine you blazing with passion," he said thoughtfully. "Some women are born cold, I expect."

She closed the door sharply behind her and went to her room before he could see the tears that refused to be held at bay any longer.

Two days later Bess and Katy made a trip into San Antonio. Joske's, where Jude had set up an account, was one of the biggest department stores in town, crammed full of delicious clothes and accessories. Bess, determined to make the best of the situation, threw herself into trying to decide what she wanted. Katy looked bored with the whole thing, and wanted to stay out in the parking lot across the street with Bandy, who'd been volunteered to drive them to town.

"But I have to have help," Bess had protested. "It's partly your wedding, too. After all, you're going to be bridesmaid."

That had caught the young girl's interest momentarily, but after Bess had worked her way through half the dress department, Katy was getting restless.

One of the salesladies finally suggested a dress with a Mexican flavor, a gauzy white creation with hand-crocheted lace around the neck and the short puffy sleeves and around the bottom. It was like a peasant dress, but exquisite. Perfect. When Bess tried it on and posed for Katy, the young girl caught her breath.

"Blondes sure look good in white," Katy said with a smile. "Gosh, you're pretty, Bess!"

"Thank you, darling. Now," she said, "next we've got to find something for you."

Katy protested loudly, but Bess was stubborn. Finally, more to get out of the store than for any other reason, Katy decided on a frilly blue dress. Bess bought her a pale blue velvet ribbon to wear with it, and white shoes and a dainty bag and gloves.

"Everybody will laugh at me," Katy wailed.

"Not in church," Bess assured her. "Besides, it's going to be in one of the old missions."

Katy frowned slightly. "It is?"

"Your father said so."

"Well." Katy brightened. "It might not be too bad after all."

I hope, Bess said silently. She couldn't imagine herself and Jude ever getting along together. She wondered how Katy was going to react to living in a constant state of war. But oddly enough, the little girl seemed to be more amused than disturbed by the warring adults.

"What did you buy?" Jude asked that afternoon when he came back from a budget meeting at a college where he was a trustee.

"A white Mexican dress," Katy said before Bess could. "And I have to wear a blue one with—yuck—lace," she added miserably. "Gosh, couldn't I wear my boots and jeans?"

"Afraid not, tiger," Jude said. "But you can always put them on after it's over."

"I guess." She got up from the table. "Well, I'd better get my homework done, I guess. I hate school. Can't I quit?"

"Sure," Jude agreed. "When you're eighteen or get your diploma, whichever comes first."

Katy stuck out her tongue at him and went upstairs.

"Show me the dress," Jude said unexpectedly.

"I'll bring it down."

"Wear it."

She glared at him. "It's bad luck."

He drew in a deep breath. "I guess having to marry you is all I need of that," he replied.

She raised her hand and hesitated.

"Go ahead," he said with an insolent smile, staring at her. "But you won't like how I get even."

Her hand fell and she left. He was still drinking coffee when she came back down with the dress over one arm. She held it up to herself and let him scan it with cold, hard eyes.

"White?" he scoffed, his green eyes piercing.

Her chin rose. "I do realize that in this permissive age, anything goes. But I still have the right to a white wedding gown, and I'm wearing one."

He frowned slightly, searching her eyes. "You're a virgin?"

"Well, don't faint," she said curtly. "There are a few of us left!"

"I suppose I should have realized it," he sighed. "You're so damned controlled."

"Said the pot to the kettle," she agreed. Her eyes ran up and down him coldly. "Thank God, I don't have to sleep with you."

She turned to leave the room, but he was on his feet before she completed the motion. He caught her arm and jerked her around with a grip hard enough to hurt, and pulled her so close that she could see the dark green circles around his pale green irises.

"Push a little harder, society girl," he said harshly, "and see what happens."

"You're hurting me," she whispered, shaken by the sudden, vicious motion of his fingers.

"You cut, too, in your own way," he replied. His nostrils were flared with anger, and his eyes were glittering in a way that was a little frightening.

"You started it," she said childishly, clutching the wedding dress in one hand.

He sighed heavily and the hand on her arm slackened a little. "I guess I did." He searched her face for a long time. "You set me off, Bess. You always have."

"I do realize that you'd rather die than have to marry me," she said tightly. "I hope you realize that the same thing goes for me, double. But it might be a good idea for Katy's sake to try and get along."

"I am," he said.

"With me!"

"That presents a problem." He noticed his hand on her upper arm and seemed fascinated with it. He drew his fingers softly down to her elbow, feeling the warmth of her skin, and he frowned. "My God, you're thin."

"It's fashionable," she said tightly, disturbed by that slow, caressing motion that he seemed hardly aware of.

"So is sex," he returned, catching her eyes. "But you haven't followed the crowd in that respect. If you're telling the truth." He dropped her arm. "Frankly, it doesn't matter to me one way or the other, since I'll never be concerned with your virtue—or your lack of it. This is a merger."

"So cold-blooded, Mr. Langston," she said under her breath, her pride stinging at what he'd said. "And so hard. You're a rawhide man."

"Sticks and stones, lady," he said carelessly. "By the way, Katy doesn't like going to bed at eight." He must have noticed the new hours Bess had implemented.

"She told me so."

He lifted an eyebrow. "But she's still doing it."

"As you said once, she likes me," she told him smugly.

He started to speak but she glared until he

changed his mind. He jerked off his tie and opened the top button of his shirt with a hard sigh. "Want a drink, debutante?"

"I don't—"

"Drink," he said for her, glancing over his shoulder. "I should have remembered that. No booze, no sex, no bad habits . . . all the virtues of a saint." He wandered off into his study without another word and closed the door.

Without understanding her own actions, she picked up a small earthenware pot from a planter in the hall and threw it straight at the center of the door. It disintegrated with a pleasingly loud smash.

Jude jerked open the door and glared at her, his eyes falling to the polished wood floor. His eyebrows rose. "Planting a garden? Aren't you a few months early and in the wrong spot?"

"I know something I'd like to plant," she returned, and her eyes measured him from head to toe. She draped the wedding gown across the banister and bent to pick up the shards of pottery.

He bent to help her and their heads collided. He caught her shoulders to stop her from pitching over backward and held her in front of him. She looked into his eyes at point-blank range and time exploded.

She could feel his breath on her mouth, he was so close; she could smell the expensive cologne he wore. It was like a dance. They both rose together to their feet, with his lean, hard hands gripping her shoulders. His eyes searched hers, and his thumbs made wild patterns on the insides of her shoulders as they moved involuntarily, finding the smooth skin under the beige top she'd bought to go with matching slacks.

His darkening eyes went slowly down to her mouth as hers went to his. His lips parted and she could see their chiseled perfection, the hard, firm lines of them with the faint darkness above the upper one where he needed a shave. It was exciting to feel his breath mingling with her own, to see his mouth so close to hers. For a long, long time she'd wondered how it would feel if he kissed her. Part of her had feared it, but another part was hungry for it.

His hand suddenly caught the thick bun of her hair and pulled her head back. His eyes glittered down at her; his nostrils flared. He was watching her mouth with an unblinking intensity, and his fingers on her shoulder and in her hair were hurting. But she could feel the long, hard line of his body against hers and it fired a hunger she'd never felt before. Just the touch of him made her weak and shaky, and she couldn't get her breath. He couldn't either, if his raspy breathing was any indication. He muttered something and abruptly bent his head.

But even as his mouth was opening to take hard possession of her own, Katy's voice burst out from the top of the staircase. "Holy cow, what happened?"

Jude jerked as if he'd been hit, almost throwing

Bess away from him. She turned and picked up her wedding gown, feeling shaken and confused and more than a little angry at her own responses.

"Your mother-to-be was planting flowers," Jude said curtly. He turned and went back into his study with a hard, dark glare at Bess. As if it were her fault, she thought wildly.

Aggie came in, and Bess ran for it, dress in hand and watched by a giggling Katy.

Bess kept out of Jude's way the next day, but he was at home and his eyes watched her accusingly. She knew he wasn't going to let her escape so easily, but she still wasn't quite prepared for what happened. Katy had gone out to groom her calf and Aggie was working on lunch when Jude strode angrily into the living room where she was busy addressing invitations for the wedding.

"There's something you and I need to get straight," he said, ramming his hands into the pockets of his slacks, looking so darkly handsome that she hated the sight of him. "I don't like having flowerpots flung at my head."

She felt the accusation all the way to her toes and her body tingled when she met his eyes.

"I beg your pardon?" she asked stiffly.

"Don't be haughty, it won't wash." He moved closer, so that he was looming over her. "You threw that pot deliberately."

"So what if I did?" she said curtly.

"I need your damned shares in my corporation. That's why we're getting married, remember?"

"That's why you're getting married," she said, straightening as pride came to her rescue. "I'm getting married for Katy."

He nodded slowly. "Okay. Let's leave it like that. No complications."

"I . . ." She dropped her eyes to his chest, where the gray patterned knit shirt he wore strained across his powerful muscles. Under it was a shadow, and she wondered absently if he was hairy or smooth there.

"You what?" he asked.

"I didn't mean that to happen, out in the hall. You just make me so mad, Jude," she said helplessly, looking up into his eyes.

"We've always made sparks together," he agreed. His eyes narrowed. "But it's got to stop."

"Then quit baiting me," she returned. "Treat me like a human being instead of some festering thorn."

"Is that how I treat you?" he asked. "I thought I was being kind. For me," he added with a hard laugh.

"I don't imagine you can help being the way you are," she said quietly, avoiding his eyes.

"Do you think you understand me, miss debutante?" he asked with a mocking laugh. "By all means, tell me about myself."

Her eyes met his and went back to her list. "I wouldn't presume that far."

"I don't have much respect for women, if that's what you meant," he said, bending his head to light a cigarette. "Katy's mother taught me a lot about them."

"All the bad things and none of the good," Bess argued. "And how could you tell Katy that her mother was a . . ." She cleared her throat.

"Can't you say the word? Would it soil your elitist tongue to say it?" he taunted.

"Anyway, it was cruel to say it in front of Katy. A girl needs at least the illusion of a mother, and you've robbed her of hers," she returned. "She's dead, after all; she can't harm Katy."

"Her memory could," he said flatly, his eyes glittering. "I won't discuss Elise with you."

"I'm not asking you to," she said, avoiding his gaze. "But it would be kind if you could stop saying horrible things about her to Katy."

"I can't talk to you," he ground out. "Everything I say winds up being defensive."

"Pardon me for breathing," she said calmly.

"Damn you . . . !"

She jerked at the hot whip of his deep voice, and pushed herself back into the cushions, crushing the list she was following in one hand.

He took a deep drag from the cigarette. "You make my blood run hot," he said savagely. "I've never in my life wanted to hit a woman as much as I'd like to hit you, so don't press your luck!"

She didn't say a word. In that white-hot anger, he was more frightening than ever. She sat, stiff-backed, and tried not to back down.

He studied her pale face for a long time. "You're

afraid of me, aren't you?" he asked suddenly. His eyes narrowed. "Yes, I think you are. That's why you're so much on the offensive with me. Offense is the best defense, is that how you see it?"

He saw altogether too much. He rattled her. She put the list aside and stood up, moving quickly out of his reach. "I need to help Aggie," she said nervously.

"No, you don't. You just need to run off and hide."

Her lower lip trembled betrayingly as she looked at him from the safety of the door. "I'll be careful to keep my thoughts to myself from now on," she said with dignity. "Will that satisfy you?"

He frowned and studied her. "You are afraid," he said, as if it shocked him.

She turned and ran out the door, slamming it quickly behind her.

After that, he was strangely quiet around her. But watchful, and faintly calculating. It made her more nervous than ever.

Meanwhile, she was reacquainting herself with the ranch and loving every mile of its awesome spread. Katy had told her that wildflowers bloomed profusely in the spring—Bess had never been there at that time of year—bluebells and Indian paintbrush and Indian blanket, prickly poppies on the cactus, and maypop and lantana. There would be beautiful yellow black-eyed Susans with black centers, and Mexican hats with their festive yellow-fringed red petals around tall black centers.

Right now, though, it was winter and nothing was blooming except Bess's growing but reluctant attraction to Jude. She found herself staring at him when he didn't see her, her eyes glued to his tall, powerful figure as he walked around the ranch and the house. It was growing increasingly harder not to stare at him over the dinner table. And all the time, he looked at her with that strange, calculating expression.

On their wedding day, she dressed in the white gown, but with all her uncertainties showing in her eyes. Was she doing the right thing? Was it sane to let him force her into a marriage that might destroy her? She was afraid of him, all right, but not for the reasons he thought. She was afraid because she wanted him. That wild encounter in the hall had shown her just how much she wanted him. But he didn't want anything from her except her shares. He'd made that perfectly clear. Could she risk living in such close proximity to him and go from day to day without letting everything she felt show? He was shrewd, and he could read rocks, much less Bess. And if he found out, every time they argued he would taunt her with her weakness for him.

She almost went downstairs and backed out of it. But it was far too late. The guests, friends of Jude's and members of the Langston family, were already waiting for them at the little Spanish mission outside San Antonio. So what could she do but go through with it and hope for the best?

But she felt empty in a way even her mother's

death hadn't made her feel. To live with a man like Jude was going to be a daily ordeal. One she was already half dreading, half anticipating as she gathered the bouquet of white and pink silk roses Katy had chosen, and went down the staircase.

4

~~~~~~~~~~~~

The mission San Jose y San Miguel de Aguayo lived up to its nickname, the Queen of Texas missions. The towering, imposing stone structure had a grace of design and a sense of history that made Bess tingle as she entered it on the arm of Jude's neighbor Adam Teague, a towering gray-headed man she'd known for years who'd agreed to stand in for Bess's late father.

There were red and white poinsettias all around the altar, and it was truly the season for them with Christmas only two weeks away. Bess had almost asked Jude to postpone the ceremony until then, but he was impatient to gain control of the shares and she'd known he'd only refuse.

He'd hired Mexican mariachis to provide an even more Spanish flavor to the ceremony, and Bess thought she'd never heard anything so beautiful as the "Wedding March" played on dozens of throbbing, romantic guitar strings. The music echoed harmonically in the interior of the church as Bess walked stiffly beside Teague to the altar under the vaulted ceiling and dome. The three vaults of the nave were outlined in beautiful, rich hues, but Bess's eyes never saw them, riveted as they were to Jude's tall figure in a somber blue pinstriped suit with a white carnation in the lapel. Her heart leapt wildly as his head turned and he stared at her with cold green eyes.

In spite of the romantic setting, he was hating every minute of this. His eyes told her so.

Teague left her beside Jude and sat down. Bess stood rigidly at Jude's side, trembling, and only half heard the brief ceremony. She was only vaguely aware of Katy standing up with them, of the faint movements of the guests in the pews. There was a smell of stone and dust and the days when this mission was a bastion of civilization in an uncivilized land. The words the minister spoke echoed around the interior of the church, as other vows must have echoed over the two centuries of the mission's existence.

Jude slipped a ring onto her finger. More words were spoken. She said two of them. Jude bent to touch his cold mouth to her lips in their first kiss as man and wife—so removed from the heated confrontation in the hall when he'd looked as if he'd kill for her mouth. And they were married.

She heard the mariachis begin to play as Jude

led her out to the church steps where the guests were waiting with rice. The rice stung. She was cold because the beautiful white dress wasn't meant for warmth on a cool December day. But she laughed and pretended that it was the happiest moment of her life as she crawled into the black Mercedes with Jude and Katy. They drove toward home, and her eyes turned back for a last glimpse of the mission complex. Now that it was all over, she wished she could go back and really see the historic shrine.

"We'll come back again someday and you can see the rose window, Bess," Katy promised. She blushed. "I mean, Mother."

Bess caught her breath as she looked over the seat at Katy, whose face was radiant. "I like that," she told the young girl with affection. "Oh, I like that very much; it sounds just right."

"It sounds absurd," Jude snapped, glaring at both of them. "She isn't your mother."

Katy's lower lip trembled and she looked down. "Yes, sir." Her eyes went to Bess. "Congratulations anyway . . . Bess."

"Thank you," Bess said, ignoring Jude's deliberate cruelty. There would be plenty of time later to tell the sweet man what a crude, unbearable, insensitive ass he was.

But in the days that followed, Jude made a point of staying away from the house. If he saw Bess at all, it was rarely, and he made no attempt to come near her at night. Apparently he'd meant exactly what he'd said about their marriage. It was to be a merger, period, with no intimacy of any kind. Bess was almost relieved; it prevented any more of the horrible confrontations that had occurred before their wedding. With plenty of time on her hands, she concentrated on preparations for Christmas.

"We never have a tree or anything," Katy said sadly when Bess started talking about where to put one. "There's no Santa Claus, so Daddy says it's just a bunch of nonsense."

Bess was horrified. She stood in the middle of the floor gaping at Katy. "But, darling, don't you know what Christmas means?"

Katy shifted uncomfortably. "The teacher tells us about it," she murmured.

"But don't you go to church on Christmas Eve and . . . ?"

Katy looked even more uncomfortable. "Daddy says—"

"Daddy says entirely too much," Bess burst out, dark eyes flashing. "Now, Katy, we're going to have a tree and presents, at least from each other," she said firmly. "And you and I are going to the Christmas Eve service at church, whether or not your father goes with us. And Aggie and I are going to fix a turkey with all the trimmings, and we're going to have Christmas."

Katy's eyes sparkled and she burst out laughing. "Oh, Bess, you make it sound so wonderful." Then the smile faded and became bittersweet. "But Daddy won't let you, I'm afraid."

"We'll see," she said firmly. "Now." She turned her attention back to the living room and pursed her lips. It was a massive room, and there were double windows facing the porch, which in turn faced the road. "We'll put it right there," she decided, "so that it can be seen outside. Do you have ornaments or decorations?"

Katy shook her head.

Bess frowned. "Haven't you ever had a tree?"

Katy shook her head again.

She'd barbeque Jude, Bess decided. Over an open pit on Christmas day with an apple in his mouth. "We'll go to the store, then," Bess said. "Get a sweater. After I speak to your father, I'll get one of the cowboys to drive us into town to get a tree and ornaments and things."

"You will?"

"I certainly will." Bess pulled on Jude's leather jacket and went out to find him.

She found him in the barn talking with one of his men, and Bess waited patiently until he finished, enjoying the nip in the air.

He came out a minute later, wearing dark slacks with a white pullover sweater and a sheepskin jacket that must have cost the earth. He stopped in the act of lighting a cigarette and stared at Bess.

"Did you want something, Mrs. Langston?" he asked with deliberate sarcasm, his green eyes alive with it.

"Yes, Mr. Langston, I did," she said imperturbably. "I want you to have someone drive us to town so that I can buy a Christmas tree and something to go on it."

"No," he said coldly. "Not in my house."

She had realized already that it was going to take a fight. She was prepared. She lifted her head with the blond hair coiled haughtily atop it and stared at him.

"Before we married, you agreed we should try to get along, didn't you?" she asked. "I haven't asked anything of you up until now. Not one single thing. But now I want half the living room. In fact, I want the half that faces the road. It has a double window. Then," she added, watching his eyebrows slowly go up in astonishment, "I want a tree—something bushy, I don't care what kind—and some ornaments and a turkey and a ham."

"Are you going to put the turkey and ham on the tree?" he asked.

She glared at him. "I also want you to buy something for Katy to go under the tree. A present that you pick out yourself, not that your secretary runs out to get on her lunch hour."

He took off his hat and idly brushed it against his leg while he looked at her. "Anything else?"

"No. That's all."

He searched her eyes and laughed shortly. "You've said your piece, now I'll say mine. Christmas is for featherbrains who haven't anything better to do . . ."

"You hush!" she said under her breath. "You know very well what Christmas is and why we celebrate it, and shame on you for spoiling it for Katy! How do you think she feels when all the other children are telling her about their Christmases and all their presents and going to church together to thank God for them? What do you suppose she says?"

He looked stunned for an instant. "It's only another day," he said defensively.

"Not to a little girl without a mother," she said quietly, and felt her own loss keenly at that moment.

He drew in a heavy breath. "All right, damn it," he bit off. "Have a tree. Have a turkey. But don't expect to drag me to church, because I won't go."

"Don't worry," she returned hotly, "I wouldn't want to have to be seen with you anyway!"

She was turning on her heel when he caught her arm and jerked her back.

"Where are you going for the tree?"

She swallowed. He was much too close. "I don't know."

His hand loosened, became slowly caressing on the leather sleeve. "You've got Katy all het up about this, I suppose," he growled.

"She only wants what other children have."

"All right. I'll drive you to town."

She turned, gaping up at him. "I . . . I thought I'd ask one of the boys. I didn't expect you to go."

His eyes searched hers slowly. "Don't you want me to?"

She couldn't answer him. Her gaze caught in his and couldn't free itself. For a long, hot moment they stood in the cold and just looked at each other.

"Hell, if we're going, let's go," he said irritably, throwing her arm away. "Get Katy." He slammed his hat over his eyes and stalked off toward the garage.

It was astonishing that he'd agreed to it. All the way to town, Bess cast curious glances his way.

"I need to run by the office for a few minutes," he said after the silent drive into town. "I'll leave you both downtown and let you shop. Meet me in front of the Menger Hotel at three."

"Yes, sir," Bess said smartly.

He glared at her as she clambered out with a giggling Katy, and his eyes promised retribution in the near future. Bess gave him her sweetest smile and blew him a kiss. That really set him off; he left rubber behind when he accelerated.

"The police will get him if he does much of that," Bess said smugly.

"He never has before," Katy murmured with a teasing smile. "My, my, he sure is strange since you came."

Bess laughed, impulsively freeing her hair from its bun and letting it fall around her shoulders. "It's nice out today, kind of like autumn." She frowned. "What am I saying, it is autumn until the twentieth, isn't it?"

"Everybody thinks of December as winter," Katy said. "Bess, is he really going to let us have a tree?" she added excitedly.

"Yes, he is," Bess said, without adding what a fight it had been. "Now. Let's get busy."

She and Katy bought boxes of ornaments and tinsel and a tree stand and skirt with the wad of bills

Jude had pushed into her purse. She sent Katy into a bakery to get breads and cookies, and while she was gone Bess quickly bought some items that the little girl had expressed a desire for. Before she could regret it, she added a new model of pocket computer that Jude had been muttering about, along with a nasty-looking tie that he was sure to hate. On Christmas morning she'd decide which of the presents to give him, she promised herself.

Jude picked them up in front of the historic old hotel near the Alamo at three, and Bess glanced hopefully down the street toward the building.

"Not today," he said flatly. "I've got a budget meeting tonight. We'll only have time to buy the damned tree and go home."

Katy looked sad, but Bess smiled over the seat at her. "You and I will go another time, okay?"

The car jerked suddenly and he gave her a look that would have stopped traffic, but she turned away and ignored it.

"So brave, aren't we?" he murmured as he flicked on the radio.

It was playing a particularly mournful song about lost love, with a line that was repeated to the point of madness: "I feeeyul sooo sick in mah heart for you."

Bess lifted her eyebrows and smiled at Jude.

"What are you grinning about?" he challenged.

"I feeyul sooo sick in mah heart for you," she drawled off-key, and Katy rolled over in the back seat, muffling her laughter.

One corner of Jude's mouth actually curled up as

he glanced at Bess. He'd stopped at a traffic light, and his lean hand shot out to catch a strand of her loosened hair and jerk it roughly.

"Thorn in my flesh," he muttered, letting go when she squealed. "Life was so peaceful until I got tangled up with you."

She pushed back the long hair that he'd tugged. "Is that what you call it? I was thinking you were probably just bogged down in bad temper."

"Careful, lady," he cautioned as he lit a cigarette. "Eventually, you'll be unprotected."

She knew what he meant, but there was a wild sweet recklessness in taunting him.

"You don't scare me, masked man," she replied. "My ancestors survived carpetbaggers and reconstruction. I reckon I can survive you."

"Out here we had Apaches and Comanches," he said, glancing at her. "As a matter of fact, my grandmother was a full-blooded Apache woman."

That explained his black hair and dark complexion and high cheekbones, she thought, studying him.

"Yes, it shows, doesn't it?" he asked. "We've got photographs of some distant cousins. Get Katy to show them to you."

"Oh, yes," Katy agreed, all eyes, "and there's a bow and arrow, and a skinning knife and a buffalo robe!"

"I used to read a lot about Cochise and the Chiricahua Apaches," Bess volunteered. "Western history was Dad's passion. He had books full of old photos of the war chiefs. Some of them were beautiful," she recalled, memories of those sculpted, proud features flashing through her mind. Involuntarily her eyes were drawn to the smooth skin of Jude's face, with the faint shadow of new beard around his mouth and chin.

He lifted an eyebrow at her. "Some Apache men took white women for their lodges, you know."

She turned back to her window. "There's a Christmas tree lot over there," she said quickly. "Could you stop?"

He pulled into the side street and parked the car. Katy ran ahead of the adults to the small dirt lot where pine and spruce trees were displayed.

"This is stupid," Jude growled out of earshot of the civic club men who were operating the lot. "Why buy a tree when we've got thousands on the ranch?"

She looked up at him. "Because the money goes to provide Christmas for children who wouldn't have any otherwise," she said gently. "Suppose Katy lived like some of the families whose houses we drove past to get here, Jude?"

His eyes lowered to hers and that same odd, penetrating look was back in them again. It made her feel trembly all over.

"Money doesn't bring happiness," she continued, "I realize that all too well. But the lack of it can cause a lot of misery."

He shifted his broad shoulders uncomfortably and glanced toward Katy, who was signaling wildly. "She's found one she likes." He glared down at Bess. "You'll have to decorate the damned thing."

She beamed. "I like decorating trees. We bought all sorts of things to put on it."

"Yes, I know," he said with a rare smile. "A turkey and a ham."

She laughed gaily, and it changed her eyes. They were filled with warmth, and her creamy complexion glowed. She tossed her head, and her silver gold hair caught the sunlight and shone like metal. Jude stared at her for a long time before he moved abruptly and went to join Katy.

The tree the little girl wanted was a huge pine over eight feet tall. Jude tried to steer her toward something smaller, but it was the only tree she wanted and she wouldn't change her mind. So Jude gave in, growling a little, and handed the man with the cashbox a large bill. Bess and Katy had gone back to the car because the wind was coming up and it was cold. But Bess glanced back in time to see Jude refusing any change, and she wanted to cry. It was just a little victory, but it was solid gold.

Jude put the tree into the stand for them and set it up; then he glared at both of them and went into town for his meeting, announcing that he'd have dinner there before it started.

Bess giggled, and Aggie came in with a puzzled frown. "He never eats in town," she sighed. "I do not understand."

"He's in a snit," Bess explained, laughing at the older woman's puzzled expression. "He's furious because he had to buy us a tree."

Aggie laughed. "But such a magnificent tree!"

she exclaimed, sighing over it as she dried her hands on her apron. "Of course, at home we always made a *nacimiento*—a nativity scene. But the tree is lovely, too."

"We bought a little nativity scene, though, Aggie," Katy told her excitedly. "And we got lights, and all sorts of stuff! I have to call Deanne and tell her!"

She ran off and Bess sighed, smiling, as she studied the huge tree. "She's been like that all afternoon," she confided. "So happy and excited. I could have cried."

"The men tell me the señor has never liked to see celebrations, señora," Aggie said sadly.

"Well, we're having one this year," Bess said shortly. "I insisted. We're even going to have turkey. And a ham, and all sorts of trimmings. I have a recipe book—I had a recipe book," she added on a sigh. "I know, I'll call the caretaker and have him send it out here express mail!"

"You have sold your home?" Aggie asked.

"Oh, no. I had Jude hire a caretaker for it," she said. "It's been in my family for a hundred years; I just couldn't sell it. It was part of the marriage contract. I gave him his blessed shares, and I got my home. And part of the living room," she added, glancing toward the tree. "He said he wouldn't have it in his house. I figure part of the house belongs to me now that we're married, so I told him I wanted half the living room."

Aggie laughed. "Señora, you have him on his head. I have never seen him so confused. He curses all the time. But I have seen him smile when he looks at you. A true smile, that of a man who is pleased with what he has.''

That was shocking. Bess had to restrain herself from pumping Aggie about her remark. But she didn't dare hope. Jude was determined to keep her at a distance, so she'd better not expect very much from him.

She and Katy decorated the tree, finishing just before Katy's bedtime. When Bess plugged in the lights, the young girl stared at it as if she'd never seen anything so beautiful. She hugged Bess hard.

''I love you,'' she choked out, and then ran away before Bess could reply.

She stood watching the tree with tears in her eyes. Who'd have thought it would mean so much to the little girl? She thought about Christmases when she was a child, and the trouble her mother and father had gone to to make them special for her. The tears rolled slowly down her cheeks. They'd been such a happy family, so happy. Then her father had died and her mother had married Crystal's father, and Bess's fragile happiness had collapsed. She couldn't help feeling sad about the past. It had been so lovely to have a family, to be part of that warmth. That was why she wanted to make it beautiful for Katy. A little girl should have some sweet memories to look back on when she grew up.

It was midnight when Bess went up to bed, and Jude hadn't yet come home. She was still amazed that he'd agreed to her demands. But, then, he was full of surprises, and she wasn't certain yet that he wouldn't get even with her for forcing his hand. Maybe Katy's expression on Christmas morning would be enough to stall him.

As it turned out, Jude didn't make any snide remarks about the tree; in fact, he pretended it wasn't there at all. But she saw him bring in a big, bulky package one night before Christmas and take it upstairs without saying a word about it to anyone. And suddenly her heart soared with happiness for Katy.

The only unpleasant note in the week before Christmas was a card from Crystal, saying that she'd only just gotten Bess's note about the wedding and would come to spend the holidays with her and Jude. That was enough to spoil the spirit of anticipation that was building inside Bess. Crystal was all she needed right now, to shatter the delicate truce she was establishing with Jude.

She could have cried. Crystal had always taken things from her. Crystal, who was beautiful and fragile and spoiled. But Bess had never minded losing before. Now it was a different story. She had Katy and at least the hope of some kind of relationship with Jude if she was patient. What if Crystal decided she wanted Bess's new husband? A black cloud settled over the holiday preparations, like the despair of the days before Bess's mother had died. She felt old suddenly, and afraid.

5

~~~~~~~~~~~~~~

What in hell is this supposed to be?" Jude asked Bess as she was setting the table for supper on Christmas Eve.

She glanced at the gracefully folded napkin beside his plate. "It's a napkin," she told him.

He glowered at it, and abruptly lifted it in his lean hand and shook it out. "If it's a napkin, suppose you let it look like one! This isn't your plantation, little Georgia peach."

She glared at him. "You'll find napkins done that way in elegant restaurants all over the country," she said with deliberate sarcasm. "If you'd rather wipe your mouth on your sleeve . . ."

His eyes flickered with a burst of emotion. "Like a savage?" he taunted. He threw the napkin down onto his plate. "That's what you've always consid-ered me, Bess. From the early days."

"That's not at all true," she said quietly. She stopped lining up silverware and stood erect, her hair long and soft, floating around the shoulders of the white Victorian dress she was wearing.

"Isn't it?" he laughed shortly. He bent to crush out his cigarette in the big ceramic ashtray she'd put out for him. "Then why do you throw pots at me, and try to slap my face, and . . ."

"Jude . . . ," she said beseechingly. "Why can't we let bygones be bygones?"

"Do you really think we can ignore the way we react to each other?" he said in surprise, and even smiled a little. "My God, I can't remember the last time a woman fought me like you have."

The remark brought embarrassing pictures to mind—Jude with a woman. She'd never thought about him in bed with a woman before, and it shocked her. Unfortunately, the shock was quite visible to his piercing gaze.

"That isn't what I meant," he murmured softly.

"Don't read my mind," she grumbled, turning back to her chore with fingers that trembled.

"Was I? What were you seeing in that suspicious little mind of yours? I didn't think ladies ever dwelled on such sordid subjects as sex."

She ignored the deliberate taunting. "Katy should be down any minute," she said quietly. "Please don't make fun of the dress I bought her to wear to the Christmas Eve service at church to-night."

He looked frankly insulted. "I never make fun of my daughter."

"Our daughter," she said coolly, staring at him.

A corner of his chiseled mouth curled upward. "Excuse me. *Our* daughter."

She finished arranging the silverware. "And would you say something nice about the way she looks?"

"Hold it, honey," he said silkily, noticing the way her head jerked up at the careless endearment that he'd just used for the first time in their stormy relationship. "I've let you get away with murder for the past week, but there's a limit to my patience."

"Do you have any?" she asked conversationally.

His chin lifted and his eyes narrowed. "Given the right circumstances, I have quite a lot," he said in a tone that rippled along her nerves like a teasing finger.

She hated the hot surge in her cheeks and lowered her hands to rearrange one of the place settings. "That's something I'll never know about," she said.

He didn't reply, and she looked up straight into his unblinking stare.

It was like lightning striking. She couldn't have dragged her eyes away from his to save her life, and the intensity of the look they were exchanging made her tingle all the way to her toes. Jude's nostrils flared with a harsh breath and he moved abruptly, coming so close that she could smell his tangy cologne and feel the heat of him.

He slid one hand into the small of her back. The

other pressed against her cheek, and he watched her curiously while his thumb began to move slowly, sensuously, across her lips, back and forth in a rough caress that had the oddest effect on her pulse.

"Cool," he breathed, "like ice to the touch, even your mouth. I've wondered for years what it would take to unstarch you."

"Don't think . . . you could do it," she whispered shakily.

But he could see the effect his hard thumb was having on her, he could see her lips parting helplessly, feel the in and out of her breath on his chin.

"I'm a man," he said quietly. "That's something you seem to have overlooked for a long time. I have all the usual needs, and I'm no virgin."

She felt her heart beating wildly and she wanted to move away, but when she tried, that steely hand behind her brought her legs against the powerful muscles of his own.

"Stop running, I won't hurt you," he growled, watching her mouth. "Not this time, at least. I'm curious about you. I want to know why you're so damned cold with me."

"You make my life miserable," she said jerkily, "you carry me off from my home and force me into a marriage I don't want, you insult me . . . and then you have the audacity to wonder why I back away when you come toward me!"

His eyebrows lifted. "You were backing away from me long before I brought you here. Two summers ago. The summer before that."

Her eyes fell to his chiseled mouth and she tried not to want it. "I've only tried to defend myself."

"After you attacked and set me off," he agreed. He sighed quietly. "I guess I am pretty hard on you sometimes."

That admission was startling, because he'd never admitted any such thing before. She glanced up, curious.

"You don't know why, do you?" he asked, searching her eyes.

She nodded. "Because you dislike me."

He laughed shortly. "God, you're green," he murmured. "Grass green and as out of place here as hothouse orchids." He caught her chin and tilted it. "That reminds me. I want you to stop putting those damned flowers in my study. Bandy made a remark about it this morning—and about that damned tree you put in the living room. Said you were softening me up."

She gave him her most belligerent glare. "And what's wrong with that, Rawhide Man? You're so hard you can't even enjoy the simple pleasures of life."

That made him angry. "We don't need all that," he said gruffly. "Christmas trees and wreaths on the damned door . . . next, I'll find lace sewn on the edges of my damned underwear!"

The thought of it made her giggle. She put up a hand to muffle her laughter, but he caught it savagely and pressed it against his chest.

Her fingers felt the heavy rise and fall of his breathing. The hand at her back involuntarily drew her closer, and with a shock she realized that the closeness of her body was beginning to have a noticeable effect on him.

Apparently he wasn't anxious to have her know that, because he immediately loosened his hold so that several inches separated them.

His eyes went down to the slender hand resting on his white shirtfront. His own hand touched it lightly, tracing the pale blue veins on its back, running over her long fingers.

"You play something, don't you?" he asked in a deep, slow drawl. "The piano?"

"Yes," she whispered.

"You have . . . lovely hands," he murmured. His breathing was growing more ragged by the second. Slowly, almost absently, he flicked open two of the top buttons of his open-necked shirt and drew her fingers inside.

She went rigid at the feel of him, at the hair-roughened warmth and strength of the hard muscles of his chest, just below his collarbone.

His lips parted as he watched her hand against his body. He opened another button and guided her hand from one side of his chest to the other, letting her fingers rest finally on one rigid male nipple.

She hadn't realized that it happened to men the way it happened to women, and she looked up with the discovery in her eyes.

His eyes held hers for a long, static moment. He bent his head just enough for her lips to come within reach of his, and she could feel the banked-down fire in him like an imminent explosion.

"Open your mouth, and fit it to mine," he whispered in a deep tone that hypnotized her.

She obeyed him in silence, a thick silence that throbbed with new emotions, new knowledge. She stood up on her tiptoes, staring at his mouth, and opened hers very slowly.

Holding her breath, she fitted her lips exactly to his hard, open mouth, and a gasp caught in her throat at the exquisite sensations that rippled through her body.

His breath mingled with hers, coming quick and harsh. Both his hands moved to her waist and lifted her gently up against his hard body while his mouth slowly increased its intimate pressure.

Her hands, both of them exploring his hard chest now, tangled in the thick mat of hair over the warm muscles and pulled, like a kitten kneading a soft cover in pure pleasure. He moaned sharply, and his mouth was suddenly demanding, hungry and re-lentless, forcing hers into a deeper union that drew a moan from her own mouth. She slid her hands up around his neck and pressed her breasts hard against his chest. She felt as though she were drowning in new and exquisite pleasures.

All at once he set her back down on her feet and stood glaring at her, his face showing mingled anger and reluctant satisfaction.

She drew away from him, surprised that he let her, and turned back to the table. "Katy . . . and I are going to services in a few minutes," she said, shaken. "Would you like to go with us?"

"No, I would not."

If she hadn't been so shaken, she might have noticed the rasping sound of his voice, the quickness of his breath, which betrayed how moved he'd been. But she didn't, and he turned away.

"I'm going out for dinner," he said coldly. "You can gush over Katy all by yourself!"

"She's your daughter, Jude," she said, her voice soft and hurt and shaking.

He stopped, his back to her, and said something rough. "I can't stay here with you," he ground out after a minute.

That was deliberately cruel, but she didn't react.

"Don't worry, Katy and I will be out of the house for at least two hours," she retorted.

"I'd still rather go to town. I've had about all the high society I can stand," he added before he slammed out the door.

She turned her back and went toward the kitchen to see how Aggie was coming with supper. But she hesitated outside the door and dried the tears that insisted on falling, no matter how hard she tried to stop them.

She put on a happy face for Katy, making some excuse about an unexpected business meeting that Jude had to attend. It pacified the little girl, but her disappointment showed. She had her long hair brushed around her shoulders, and she was wearing the ruffled pink dress Bess had bought for her.

She looked so lovely. And Jude didn't even care enough to stay and see her. Bess could have shaken him.

Later, when it was bedtime, Katy came into Bess's room and they sat in their nightgowns on Bess's bed while the older woman told her about Christmases at the Georgia estate where she grew up.

"Do you miss your mother a lot?" Katy asked.

"Yes," she said. "I miss her terribly. But she was very sick and she's so much better off."

"She's in heaven," Katy said, understanding. She held Bess's hand. "You aren't sorry you came here, are you? You aren't sorry you married Daddy?"

"No, I'm not sorry," Bess said softly, and smiled. "Look what a beautiful daughter I got."

Katy blushed and grinned. "Bess, did you have parties at Christmas when you were a little girl?"

"Not a lot of them," Bess sighed. "But when my stepsister got big enough, her father insisted that she have them. She had lots of boyfriends."

"Did you?"

Bess shook her head. "No, darling. I'm very plain, you know."

"Daddy doesn't think so," Katy said. "I heard him tell Mr. Teague that you were a vision. Doesn't that mean pretty?"

"There are different kinds of visions," Bess said sadly, thinking Jude probably meant she was a nightmare. Remembering the way he'd kissed her downstairs, she went hot all over. Why had he done that?

She stretched, bringing the elasticized bodice of her nightgown precariously low, but she didn't notice. "Darling, I'm tired, and tomorrow is Christmas. Let's get some sleep," she told Katy. "Tomorrow we'll make some roasted pecans to snack on, all right?"

"All right," Katy said, getting up. "Bess, I'm so glad you came to live with us."

"So am I," Bess said, and was about to elaborate when Jude walked in.

He hadn't even bothered to knock, and he looked a little wild. His black hair was hanging untidily down on his forehead and his green eyes were hard and glittering.

"Having a party?" he asked, his voice slightly slurred.

"Just saying good night to each other," Bess said, sitting up straighter even though the action brought her bodice still lower. She felt a sense of power at the expression that went over his hard features, and she didn't follow her first impulse, which had been to pull up the slipping fabric.

"Good night, Daddy," Katy said, standing on tiptoe as he lowered his cheek so she could kiss him. "You should have come to church with us; it was lovely. The minister said I looked pretty," she added, grinning. "Night, Bess."

"Night, darling," Bess said, cringing inside when Katy went out with a wicked smile and deliberately closed the door behind her.

"Church," Jude growled. "And Christmas trees and turkeys and turning my damned house and my life upside down." He was breathing roughly, and Bess suddenly realized that he'd been drinking.

Her lips parted on a rush of breath. "The service was very nice," she said after a minute. "And Katy did . . . look lovely."

"So did you," he ground out, staring pointedly at her bodice. "All lace and ruffles . . . did you wear that thing deliberately?"

She swallowed nervously. "What thing?"

"That gown," he said, moving closer to the bed with a little less than his usual elegance of movement. He sat down heavily beside her, still staring at the gown.

"I . . . couldn't have known . . . you'd come in here," she managed through tight lips.

"Oh, of course not," he muttered, glaring at her. "But you let it slip deliberately, honey," he added with a glittering smile. "You saw my eyes on you and you liked it."

He caught both her nervous hands in one of his and locked them together over her waist, pressing her back in a sitting position against the pillows. The other hand went to the elasticized bodice, and his eyes were suddenly cruel. "If you want me to look at you, Bess, you don't have to play teenage games. Just tell me."

As he spoke, he ripped the bodice down to her waist, baring her small, taut breasts to his hot eyes.

He stared down at them as if he had every right,

letting his eyes take in each line, each soft curve, each contrast of color from soft pink to mauve.

The hand holding hers tightened as he studied her, and his face went curiously rigid, leaving only his eyes to express his churning emotions.

Bess couldn't move. His intent stare kept her still. He was looking at her in a way no man ever had before, and there was an expression in his eyes that puzzled, excited. Her breath came in unsteady gasps while sensation after sensation washed over her like flames.

Finally, finally, his eyes wandered back up to hers, to read the wonder and faint embarrassment in them.

"Yes, you do like it, don't you?" he asked curtly. "Haven't you ever been like this with a man?"

She shook her head slowly, but words were beyond her.

His eyebrows rose slightly. "Never?" he asked, as if that were incomprehensible.

"As you, yourself, said . . . my blessings are small," she said in a whisper, turning her face away.

"Don't," he breathed. He freed her hands and drew her face back to his eyes. "Don't. You're exquisitely formed, as delicate as the inside of a seashell, pink and cream . . ." He caught his breath as he looked back down at her body, his eyes fiercely possessive. "My God, I've never seen anything so sweet as this!"

He'd been drinking, of course, she told herself as she watched him. But he was making her feel things she'd never experienced, and she loved having his eyes on her. She wanted him to bend down and put his mouth there, *there*.

Her thoughts shocked her and she caught her breath.

His eyes came back up to hold hers. "We're married," he reminded her quietly. "There's no shame in this."

Her breath stopped in her throat. "Yes, I . . . I know," she said.

He reached out a gentle hand and touched her cheek, then eased his fingers into her hair. "You're so young," he said in the tenderest voice she'd ever heard him use. "So untouched by ugliness and pain. I should have had enough humanity left to keep you away from me." He drew in an angry breath and stood up, standing rigidly with his back to her as he lit a cigarette.

She lay there helpless, puzzled by words she didn't understand. "Jude?" she asked softly.

He turned, his eyes going helplessly to her soft bareness. They closed, almost painfully. "Oh, God, will you cover yourself up?" he asked under his breath as he turned away again. "I've had three neat whiskeys, Bess, and it's been months since I've had a woman."

She tugged her bodice back in place with trembling hands. "And you don't want me; you needn't bother repeating it," she said in a cool tone that hid her wounded pride.

He actually laughed, but bitterly. "You might be

89

surprised at the things I want, but I'm a realist these days. I know my own limitations."

"You, with limitations?" she scoffed, dragging the coverlet over herself. "How shocking."

He glanced back and then turned around, lifting the cigarette to his mouth as he studied her flushed face. He looked so masculine and sensuous that she wanted to climb out of the bed and throw herself at him. The way he'd looked at her body had been unspeakably beautiful, and she knew that despite the fact that he'd been drinking, she'd treasure the memory of this night forever. A kiss and then this . . . it was like having her secret longings all fulfilled at once.

"You aren't really cool at all, are you?" he asked quietly. "It's a kind of armor you wear, a form of protection."

She flushed wildly. "Stop taking me apart."

He shook his head. "I'm not doing that. You're much too complex. But, downstairs"—he watched her flush with the memory of it—"you were with me every step of the way. I hadn't expected you to kiss me, even when I told you to. I was . . . teasing."

Oh, God, she thought miserably. She closed her eyes and drew in a steadying breath. Please, please don't let me give myself away, she pleaded silently.

"Would you mind finding some other method of torture in the future?" she asked unsteadily. "As you said yourself, I'm too green to know the difference."

"Did it hurt?" he asked, as if it mattered.

She laughed bitterly. "I wouldn't let you hurt me. Not in a million years."

He made a rough sound in his throat and crushed out his cigarette, even though he'd only finished half of it. "Damn it, what I had in mind for us was a simple merger, a marriage based on business concerns, not emotion. I haven't changed my mind. I wanted the shares, not complications."

Her eyes fell to the coverlet, which her fingers were worrying. "Then stop creating them," she said.

"Stop helping me," he shot back, glaring at her. "I'm human. I respond to temptation just like any other damned man."

"I wasn't—"

"Try again." His eyes darkened as he studied her, and she looked away because she couldn't outstare him.

"I won't forget," she said on a sigh.

"See that you don't." He paced the room angrily.

She studied the coverlet as if it fascinated her. "Jude, why haven't you ever had a Christmas tree before?"

He glanced at her briefly. "Because I never realized how much it meant to Katy until now." He laughed shortly. "All this time she pretended that she didn't care. And I was too damned busy." He lifted his chin and studied her thoughtfully. "She shines like a new penny these days. You've got her heart in your pocket. Just don't set your cap at mine, lady."

"That frozen thing?" she asked with a calm she didn't feel. "Why should I want it? Anyway, you don't want me," she added quietly.

His eyes pinned her to the bed. "I wanted you downstairs," he said, shocking her.

Her face went blood red, and he watched it with lifted eyebrows.

"My, my, what an interesting reaction," he said. "Very virginal."

"Not exactly by choice," she said coldly. "There was little opportunity for me to attract men as long as Crystal lived at home."

"Tinsel usually overshadows gold," he said thoughtfully, looking at her. "Your stepsister is beautiful, all right. Did she steal all your boy-friends?"

"Every last one."

"Then they couldn't have cared very much," he said. "It's probably better that you kept your chastity."

"It will be a great comfort to me in my old age," she agreed.

His eyes searched hers. "You won't change a lot with age, I don't think," he mused. "You have beautiful bone structure."

She returned the long, searching glance and slowly, poignantly, an idea began to form in her mind. He wasn't quite as unapproachable as he usually was. If she could find a way to capture his attention before Crystal showed up, if she could . . .

Her lips parted nervously. "Jude . . . are you . . . very tired?" she asked hesitantly.

His darkening eyes wandered slowly over her. "Are you offering me your body?"

She swallowed down a quick denial and caught her nervous fingers in the coverlet. "Do . . . do you want it?"

His chest rose and fell roughly. "Oh, yes," he said with self-contempt. "I want you."

She stood up, feeling wildly reckless and inhibited at the same time. She forced herself to face him. Her fingers went to the gown and slowly, deliberately, eased it down her waist, over her smooth hips and onto the floor.

Jude stared at her as if he'd never seen a woman in his life. His face flushed slightly, and his eyes exploded with a desire that darkened them almost to black.

"Grace and elegance," he breathed. "I imagined you'd be proud even when you offered yourself. You are so lovely, Bess," he added with deep emotion. "So lovely. Don't tempt me, honey. I'm hungry and it's been a long time."

He started to turn away, but she touched his arm, daring everything.

"Would . . . would it be so hard?" she whispered, her voice shaking with embarrassment.

"No." He shook his head. "Quite the contrary. But if you got pregnant . . ."

Her face brightened, changed, and her eyes softened. "Oh, I'd like that," she breathed. "I'd like being pregnant with your baby."

He actually trembled. "Bess . . ."

"Don't you want a son, Jude?" she asked, looking up with her whole heart in her eyes.

He reached for her, crushing her bareness to every hard line of his body, burying his face in her soft hair.

"Yes," he ground out achingly. "I want a son. I want you. But . . ."

"But what?"

His fingers tightened at her back. "Bess, you know that I served in Vietnam, that I saw combat?"

"Yes."

He sighed heavily. "My unit ran into an ambush, and I caught a lot of shrapnel. My right hip and thigh look like a road map of the moon. The scars have faded some over the years, but I've had women ask me to put out the light. . . ."

He laughed when he said it, but Bess ached for his pride. How it must have hurt!

"I won't ask you to put out the light," she said into his ear. "I wouldn't care if you were missing an arm or a leg . . . you'd still be Jude!"

He caught his breath at the admission and she felt a shudder work its way through him. "You may regret this in the morning," he ground out.

"I'll worry about it in the morning. Jude, please . . . ?"

"Good God, you don't have to beg. Can't you feel how much I want it?" He bent and took her mouth roughly, possessively, and she gave herself up to the wild arousal.

She felt him lift her onto the bed and she lay watching him as he undressed with jerky, urgent movements. She knew he wasn't quite sober, but at last some of the barriers were down and she was going to take full advantage of it. Her eyes didn't waver when he turned back to her; she let them linger on the white scars across his hip and thigh. He was pale there, probably because he never went swimming or wore shorts, and she could see why. It wasn't pretty, but it wasn't as horrible as he seemed to think it was. The rest of him was all hard muscle under thick black hair, and the muscles rippled when he moved. He was broad chested, narrow hipped, as graceful as a cat.

"No comment?" he asked as he slid onto the bed beside her.

"Did you expect me to faint?" she asked with a tiny smile. "I almost did, but it wasn't because of the scars."

His eyebrows arched and he made a tiny, amused sound. "Haven't you ever seen a man undressed before?"

She shook her head.

His fingers touched her mouth, her cheek. "I'll try to be careful," he said, bending to kiss her softly. "But I'm pretty rusty, Mrs. Langston. It's been a long, long time since I had a woman in my bed."

Amazingly uninhibited with him, she reached up with loving arms to hold him while he teased her mouth. She felt as if she were seeing for the first time the man beneath the hard veneer.

"I didn't think you felt . . . like this," she whispered, tautening when he touched her unexpectedly.

He lifted his head, frowning. "Why not?"

She flushed, lowering her eyes to his hairy chest. "You're always sniping at me."

"Don't get any ideas about it," he said coolly, hesitating. "I don't love you, Bess. I want you, but that's it."

She felt a cold sickness well up inside her and almost jerked away from him. But there was something different in his manner, in his eyes. She knew she wasn't going to change him overnight. She'd just have to be patient. And at least he wanted her. A child might soften him, just a little, if he could watch her grow big with it and be there in its early years—things he'd missed when Katy was born.

"I'm not asking for miracles," she said softly. "I . . . I'll try to please you if you'll tell me what to do."

His eyes closed for an instant and his lips compressed. "Damn, Bess!"

"What is it?" she asked, reaching up to smooth her fingers over his broad chest as she had done in the dining room.

Surprisingly, he turned over on his back. "Don't stop now," he said quietly.

Her hands, shy at first, smoothed over his shoulders and chest, rediscovering the different textures of skin and hair and muscle and bone. He watched her, lying back on the pillows like some Middle Eastern potentate, faintly smiling.

When her hands stopped at the powerful muscles of his stomach, just below his waist, he actually grinned at her embarrassment.

"Coward," he taunted.

She smiled back. "I'm new at this."

"You'll learn." He sat up, bringing her body against his, watching her breasts vanish in the thick hair over his chest. "Now, it's my turn," he breathed, bending to kiss a shocked gasp from her parted lips. "My turn," he growled again, easing her down onto the mattress.

She felt her body blaze up with sensation. His strolling fingers learned every silken inch of her, his lips soon following the same path. The room was utterly quiet except for the reckless sounds they made together.

Once, her eyes opened and looked straight up into his as his powerful body eased down totally against her.

"Afraid?" he whispered.

"Yes," she agreed unsteadily.

His body moved and she gasped.

"It won't ever hurt again after this," he whispered gently, controlling the motion of his powerful body with an effort that showed in every strained line of his hard face. "Is it bad?"

It was, but she shook her head, and a minute later the lie became truth. She arched helplessly and there was a sudden tenderness in his eyes as his motions grew deep and urgent and his hands taught her the strange new rhythm.

She lost track of time and place in the grip of something so exquisitely torturous that she felt as if she were dying of a particularly vicious fever. Her body burned with it, and there was no relief. She was slowly, agonizingly being stretched in a tension that would surely kill her.

"No," she whispered urgently, her fingernails clutching wildly, her teeth against his shoulder. "No, I can't!"

He was laughing triumphantly . . . laughing! His hands controlled her wild body, forcing it to comply with the demands he was imposing. And then it was all sweet explosion and consuming flames, snapping the tension, and she fell and fell and fell. . . .

It seemed like hours before she could breathe again, before her eyes stopped melting in hot tears that fell onto his damp chest. She was trembling, and so was he in the aftermath of something so volcanic that she blushed just remembering it.

His hand brought her eyes up to his and he caught his breath as he watched her. "Not what you expected, honey?" he asked softly.

"I . . . thought it would . . . hurt," she whispered.

His eyes wandered slowly down the length of her body. "Didn't it? You cried out."

She blushed wildly and hid her eyes, and he laughed again, softly. He bore her down onto the mattress with a glittering wildness in his eyes that she'd never seen in them. His nostrils flared as he breathed.

"Last time was for you," he said under his breath as his fingers moved in slow exploration. "This time," he whispered, bending to her mouth, "is for me. . . ."

The night was at once the longest and shortest she'd ever spent, and as dawn slowly erased the blackness outside the window, she ached pleasantly from head to toe. She was astounded at Jude's inexhaustible ardor. She flushed at just the memory of it and wondered at his stamina—and her own.

But the tender, hungry lover of the night was sadly lacking in the bitter-faced man who dragged himself out of bed and dressed in the dim light. She didn't remember when he'd turned the lights out.

He dragged on his shirt and flicked the light on, standing quietly in his jeans and staring at her with eyes she couldn't read.

Self-consciously, she tugged the sheet over her breasts and flushed at the intensity of his gaze.

"And now you know, don't you?" he asked with a mocking laugh. "You know that I want you to the point of obsession. But don't think you're going to put a ring through my nose because of it, honey. You won't own me. Not even if you give me a child out of last night. I hope you meant what you said about wanting that baby, Bess, because I'm through keeping my distance from you. I'll have Aggie move your things into my room in the morning and you can sleep with me from now on."

She stared at him with slow comprehension. "But . . . you said you . . . wanted a child too," she reminded him.

"My God, I wanted you, you stupid woman," he ground out, glaring down at her. "I'd have agreed with anything to get . . ." He sighed and turned away, running a restless hand through his hair. "It had been months, and I was hungry for something female in my arms. All that whiskey and all the lonely nights caught up with me." His eyes glittered at her. "And you stripped off that damned gown and came at me like Venus rising. I'm human, damn you!"

She turned her head away on the pillow, her eyes closed as the tears ran freely down her cheeks. For just a few hours she'd thought he was as involved as she was, as full of wonder about what they'd shared. But it had all been a sham, like their marriage.

"Regretting it won't help now," he said coldly. "Just remember, lady, it was all your idea."

But she didn't answer him. She couldn't. Her heart was breaking in half.

He stood by the bed for a minute, and she felt that he wanted to say something. But the moment passed and he left her, slamming the door behind him.

6

~c&c&c&c&c&c&c&c~

Getting up and pretending that everything was fine was the hardest thing Bess had ever done. She put on the soft beige jersey dress that she'd come from Georgia in, and rolled her hair into a French twist at her nape. She hardly bothered with make-up because no one would see her except Jude and she didn't care how she looked anymore. She'd wanted him so much, loved him so much. She'd thought he cared a little . . . and it had all been sex.

She laughed at her own naivety. And tonight she'd sleep in his arms and it would all happen again. But her response wouldn't be as uninhibited, she promised herself. He wouldn't wring that madness from her twice, not when she knew he was hating her for "tempting" him. She picked up her brush and almost flung it into the mirror in pure fury. If only she hadn't been so stupid, so trusting. She straightened. For Katy's sake, she was going to have to put on her brightest face and pretend everything was just fine.

She went to Katy's room and knocked on the door. She peeked her head inside and smiled at the head under the covers.

"Hey," she called softly. "Santa Claus has come by now, I imagine. Want to go downstairs and see?"

Katy was instantly awake and all eyes. "Oh, let's!" she agreed, bounding out of bed to grab her quilted pink robe and slippers.

Bess put an arm around her as they went to the staircase, dreading the confrontation that would undoubtedly come with Jude.

The presents she'd put under the tree last night after she'd sent Katy upstairs were where she'd left them, but some more had been added. She frowned at the size of one of them, a big rectangular thing wrapped in brown paper with a frilly bow stuck to one corner. Perhaps Aggie had put it there.

"Shouldn't we get Daddy?" Katy asked at the foot of the stairs.

"Yes, I suppose so," Bess said halfheartedly. "Why don't you go upstairs and knock on his door, darling?"

"No need," Jude said from the hall. "I woke early."

He had a coffee cup in one hand and he was wearing jeans and nothing else. His broad, hair-covered chest was bare and so were his feet, and he looked . . . odd.

Bess couldn't meet his eyes. She went into the living room behind Katy, aware of Jude near her. It must be some sort of radar, she thought hysterically. She always knew where he was.

"I knew you'd come to watch me open my presents," Katy laughed, dragging her father to the tree. "Here, this one is yours. I hope you like it!"

Jude sprawled on the carpet and opened the package, murmuring appropriately at the special cigarette case Katy had bought him with her own money. Bess knew it was something he'd never use, but Katy had insisted.

"Oh, Dad, thank you!" Katy was cooing, as she opened a present that contained an automatic camera and film and flashcubes. "You remembered!"

"It was hard to forget," he murmured drily, and Bess almost laughed as she recalled Katy's repeated hints every morning at breakfast.

"Aren't you going to open yours?" Jude asked Bess, glancing in her direction without actually looking at her.

"Yes, here it is, Bess!" Katy said, handing her a small present.

"That wasn't the one I meant, but go ahead and open it," he said.

Bess tore the ribbons and paper and found a bottle of her favorite cologne. She leaned forward and kissed Katy. "Thank you, darling," she said softly. "It's my very favorite."

"I hoped you'd like it. Thank you for mine," she added, hugging the musical computer that Bess had given her.

Jude reached out and tugged the big, rectangular package from its perch against the wall and handed it to Bess.

"I . . . I didn't expect anything," she said, avoiding his eyes.

"Neither did I," he said, holding up the as yet unopened package that contained the nasty tie.

She tore open the paper, and when she saw what he'd given her she couldn't say a word. Her eyes filled with tears and she chewed hard on her lower lip to keep from crying. There, in the torn folds of the wrapping paper, was the painting she'd admired that first day at the San Antonio airport— with the windmill and ranch house against the flat horizon.

"Cat got your tongue?" he taunted.

She took a slow breath. "Thank you," she said in a subdued tone, touching the painting lightly, lovingly. "I . . . I wanted it very much."

He didn't say a word, but when he started to open his gift she touched his hand lightly.

"No," she said. "That's just a tie. I have another . . ."

She jumped up and ran all the way up the stairs to take the pocket computer out of her chest of drawers. She was breathless when she got back and thrust the small package into his hands.

Puzzled, he unwrapped it with slow, deliberate

movements of his lean hands, and when he saw what it was he just stared at Bess.

"How did you know I wanted this?"

She shifted uncomfortably. "The same way you knew I wanted this, I guess," she said, touching the painting.

He was leaning back against the armchair with one leg propped up, and his eyes were calculating. Half-dressed as he was, he looked devastating.

"Well?" he said curtly.

"Well what?"

"Don't I get a kiss?" he asked with raised eyebrows. "You gave Katy one."

"You must, Bess!" Katy insisted, his willing co-conspirator, both of them ignoring the older woman's blush. "It's Christmas."

"She's shy," he told Katy. "Why don't you go get Aggie and tell her to come and open her presents?"

"Sure!" Katy laughed, leaping up to go in search of the housekeeper.

Bess flushed wildly, lowering her eyes to the carpet when they were alone.

"Shy?" he taunted. "There isn't an inch of you I don't know now."

"Oh, yes, there is," she replied, lifting her eyes. "My mind. And my heart. You don't know the first thing about either one."

"And I don't care to," he said flatly. "Your body is the only thing about you that interests me. Come here."

"Go to hell."

"It's Christmas," he reminded her, lifting his arrogant chin and smiling, but it wasn't a friendly smile. "Come here, Bess, or I'll tell Katy you don't like me."

"Go ahead, it's the truth," she said, hating him.

He leaned forward and caught her wrist, propelling her across his powerful legs and into his arms. He levered her down to the carpet, looming over her and pinning her there with his hands on her wrists.

"Fight me," he whispered with a husky laugh. "Fight me, Bess, and we'll see who wins."

She drew in an angry breath and let her eyes tell him how furious she was with him. But she stopped struggling. He seemed to like subduing her. But that was like him, too.

"That's more like it," he murmured as he bent his head. His lips were poised just above hers, so that she could feel and taste his smoky breath. "Now open your mouth the way you did last night, and let's get drunk on the taste of each other all over again. . . ."

Her mind rebelled even as her body obeyed him. She tried to be cool, not to respond, but he was hungry and she liked the roughness and power of his embrace; she liked the way it made her feel to know that he was aroused.

"Oh, yes," he breathed as he felt her shy response. "Yes, like that. Hold me, Bess."

Her arms went up around him and she felt with a sense of awe the full weight of his body on hers.

"Katy . . . ," she whispered shakily.

"I'll hear them," he whispered back. "Bess," he breathed, and she felt his hand brush from her waist up over one taut, full breast to cup and caress it while his mouth made her want to scream with its slow, taunting arousal.

His thumb was stroking her, driving her mad, and she twisted to escape it, but it followed, easing under her bra, taking fabric with it, to find the softness of her.

His eyes were wild when he drew away, glittering like green fireworks in his taut face. "We'll sleep together tonight," he breathed huskily. "I'll have you again. And again." His mouth crushed down onto hers. "Oh, God, I want you!" he groaned.

He moved, making her aware of the force of his passion, and she gasped.

"You can feel it, can't you?" he asked roughly. "A man can't hide his hungers the way a woman can. I've tasted you and now I want more, I want to make a banquet of you. You knew I would, damn you; you're just like every other damned woman . . ."

She turned her head weakly away, closing her eyes. Would he never tire of hurting her?

He rolled away abruptly and propped himself back up against the chair. He pulled a cigarette and matches down from the coffee table and lit one with fingers that weren't quite steady.

Bess sat up, straightening her hair.

"You look tidy enough," he said curtly, glaring at

her. "Nothing ruffles you very much, society girl, not even rolling around on the floor with me."

She got to her feet with exquisite grace and turned away to pick up the wrapping paper and stuff it into one of the boxes Katy's presents had come in.

"No comment?" he taunted, his voice cold and hard.

"What would you like me to say, Jude?" she asked quietly, turning to face him. "I'm vulnerable with you. I can't help it. I don't have the experience to pretend I don't like what you do to me. But it isn't kind of you to make fun of me."

He laughed shortly and averted his eyes. "But then, I'm not a kind man. I never pretended to be."

"If you hate me so much, then file for divorce," she said proudly.

"What kind of settlement would you like?" he asked with pursed lips and biting sarcasm. "An oil well or two? A new mink and a Ferrari every year?"

"I don't want money," she said, bending to pick up a stray ribbon. "I never did. I can work for what I want."

"I can see you now, waiting tables," he chided.

She stood up, regal and cool. "There's no disgrace about honest work. I could wait tables as well as anyone else. I'm not trained to do much, but I'm not afraid of hard work. Keep your money, Jude," she added with a faint smile. "I don't need it, or you."

His eyes began to glitter and he got to his feet

slowly, menacingly. "Don't you? I could make you beg for me."

She straightened. "Yes," she agreed in a small voice. "I know you could."

His hand sliced through the air, making the cigarette tip glow wildly. "Damn you! So cool and untouchable!"

"Here's Aggie," Katy called as she and the housekeeper joined them. She paused, glancing from Bess's white face to Jude's red-tinged one.

"I . . . was just telling Jude that my sister is coming to spend some of the holidays with us," Bess blurted out, flushing.

Jude's eyes widened. "Crystal?"

"Yes," she said with a nervous smile. "I meant to tell you sooner, really I did, but I kept wondering how to do it."

"I don't mind having her here," he said with a smile that only Bess saw. "She'll be a nice decoration. How long is she staying?"

"She didn't say," Bess managed.

His eyes wandered over her face. "Afraid of the competition?" he chided.

She turned away. "I've never been any competition for Crystal," she said with quiet dignity. "She takes what she likes."

Jude scowled at her, his eyes strange and intent. But he didn't say a word. He only lifted the cigarette to his lips and turned back to Katy and Aggie, who were exclaiming over the scarf Aggie had gotten from Bess and the hand-crocheted shawl she'd gotten from Jude and Katy.

Later, Jude went upstairs to dress for dinner and Katy and Bess helped Aggie set the table. It was overflowing with everything from Sally Lunn bread, which Bess had made from the old home recipe, to ambrosia and ham and turkey and dressing and giblet gravy with homemade potato rolls and Southern cornbread, cranberry sauce, green beans and mashed potatoes and sweet potato soufflé. For dessert there was fruit cake, and apple pie, and hand-dipped chocolates.

Bess forced herself to eat, even though she'd long since lost her appetite. Jude managed to put away a filled plate, but his eyes kept lancing toward Bess, and she couldn't meet them. He hated her, and she knew it. But there was nothing she could do or say in her own defense. She'd tempted him, all right. She'd wanted him desperately. She loved the horrible man, and he wanted no part of her.

Her eyes drifted down to her black coffee in its delicate china cup. Why had he bothered to buy her the painting? she wondered. Had it been for Katy's sake? To keep peace? She sighed, sounding so lonely and forlorn that everyone looked at her.

"Bess, why are you so sad?" Katy asked gently.

"Niña, the señora has no mother to celebrate this Christmas with," Aggie said gently. "We must not mind if she feels a sadness."

Bess looked at Aggie and smiled. "Thank you, but I'm coping very well. I have another family now to celebrate with."

Jude abruptly threw down his napkin and got up

from the table, strode away toward his study and slammed the door behind him.

"What's the matter with Daddy?" Katy asked, shocked.

Bess shook her head. "He doesn't like—" She almost said "me," but caught herself in time. "Christmas," she said instead. "I'm afraid it's all caught up with him."

"But he said he liked the tree," Katy told her. She grinned. "And he told me how long it took him to find the painting you wanted. It had been sold and he had to find the man who bought it to get it back."

How strange that he'd gone to so much trouble for someone he disliked. But before Bess had time to reflect on Jude's odd behavior, the phone rang. Aggie was back in a minute to get Bess.

Bess picked up the receiver, feeling a sense of impending doom because there was only one person who might be calling her today.

"Hello?" she said.

"Hello, Merry Christmas!" Crystal's bubbly voice was instantly recognizable. "Send someone to the airport to fetch me, love. I've come to cheer up your dreary holidays!"

7

The airport was bustling when Jude and Bess got there, but it only took a minute for them to spot Crystal. She would have stood out anywhere in the white satin blouse and black skirt she wore. With her exquisite face and figure and her tumble of long, straight blond hair, she was absolutely stunning.

"Darling!" she called, running straight toward Bess and Jude.

But it was Jude whose arms she ran into, and while Bess watched, horrified, Crystal kissed him on the mouth, her ardor real and sickening to watch. Worse, Jude didn't seem to mind at all. His arms contracted and he laughed as he let her go.

"Hello, bubbles," he said, grinning at the younger woman. "How long can we keep you?"

Crystal looked ecstatic, Bess thought. Already she had a captive male. And who cared that it was dry old Bess's husband, anyway? "As long as you'll let me," she told Jude, grinning gaily. "I've had a tiff with my count, and I may never leave Big Mesquite. How's that?"

Bess stood rigidly while Crystal hugged her. She was certain Crystal's affection was all for show.

"Hi, love," Crystal murmured. "Bad Christmas for you this year, isn't it, with Carla dead?"

Bess's eyes began to water and she turned away. "I'm glad you could come to visit," Bess said tautly.

Jude was glaring at her, but she didn't look his way. "You just missed Christmas dinner, but Aggie can fix you a plate," Bess said graciously, remembering her manners.

"Lord, I couldn't eat a bite!" Crystal sighed. "I had dinner on the plane, you know. Cardboard and all that, but it was filling, at least. And I never eat much. Have to watch my figure!"

So did everyone else, Bess thought uncharitably, seeing the way male eyes followed her flamboyant stepsister as they weaved through the travelers on their way to the parking lot.

"You're very quiet today, Bess," Crystal remarked when they were settled in the Mercedes— with Crystal, as Bess had expected, in the front seat and Bess in the back.

"She had a bad night," Jude said, straight-faced, and fortunately Crystal turned around before she saw Bess's wild flush.

"Well, I could have died when I read that note

about the two of you getting married," Crystal told Jude. "You used to swear you'd never let any woman get a hold on you."

"I meant it, too," he said imperturbably, lighting a cigarette. "I married Bess because of those damned shares. I couldn't get them any other way, thanks to Carla."

"Lord, she did hate you, didn't she?" Crystal laughed. "Poor Jude. Is marriage awful?"

Bess, sitting ignored in the back seat, could have shot them both. If only Jude had allowed Katy to come with them so she could have had someone to talk to!

"It has its compensations," Jude murmured, glancing in the rearview mirror. "Doesn't it, Bess?"

"Yes," she said sweetly. "Katy is one of them."

He didn't like that. His eyes glared at her. But Crystal laughed.

"That sounds like you, darling," she told her stepsister. "You always did love kids. Are you going to have some of your own?"

"Yes," Bess said curtly, and her eyes dared Jude to argue. He didn't seem to want to.

"Bess is good with Katy," he said as he turned onto the main highway. "They're already pals."

"I can't wait to see Katy again," Crystal said with a lazy smile. "She was just a baby the last time at that family get-together."

"You've missed them all for years," Jude reminded her.

"Oh, I've been busy," Crystal sighed. "Traveling, you know."

And sleeping around and such, Bess thought venomously, but she didn't say anything. She just stared out the window.

When they reached the ranch, Bess showed Crystal up to the guest room. Hoping to take advantage of the moment of privacy, she lingered while Crystal unpacked.

"Seriously," Bess asked as Crystal dropped her cosmetic bag carelessly on the bed. "How long are you staying?"

"Just a little while," came the sunny reply. "You don't mind, do you? I . . . need someplace to stay, just until I can get my life and my finances in order again."

Is that it, or are you after my husband? Bess wondered bitterly, but she was geared to keeping her worries deep inside. She fingered the door facing.

"You're welcome, of course," she said.

Crystal turned from the window and gazed at her. She made an odd little gesture with one manicured hand. "Marriage not going well?" she asked with faint humor. "Most relationships have rocky starts, darling."

Bess only stared at her. "How was Paris?"

Crystal looked haunted. "Beautiful, of course," she laughed nervously. She stared at the coverlet. "Bess, I wish . . ." She glanced toward her stepsister hopefully, but there was no softening. She shrugged. "Thanks for letting me come."

Bess turned. "Come on down when you've unpacked. Katy will be glad to see you."

"I wish you were," Crystal murmured, but her stepsister was already out of earshot.

Katy had been courteous to Crystal, but Bess sensed that the young girl really didn't like her very much.

"She's not like you at all, is she?" Katy asked later that afternoon, when the two of them were walking around the ranch yard. Crystal had pleaded with Jude to explain his computer system to her, and she'd managed to get him all to herself.

"No," Bess said, tugging her leather jacket closer. "We were never really close. We had nothing in common."

Katy sighed, snuggling closer as the wind whipped around them. "Bess, are you going to have some babies?"

"I hope so," she replied. She glanced down. "Will you mind?"

"Oh, no," Katy said honestly. "I'd like to have a baby to help take care of. I like babies. They smell nice."

Bess laughed, daydreaming about how it would be to have a little pink baby to hold and kiss and share with Katy and . . . The smile faded. Jude hadn't really meant it about wanting one. He'd only wanted Bess and had been ready to say anything to get her.

"Want to go watch Blanket eat?" Katy asked. "She's working out real well, Bandy says. She's going to be a good saddle horse."

"If she ever stops falling on people," Bess laughed. "Sure, let's go look."

Blanket was munching oats when they walked down the long, wide aisle between the hay-filled stalls. She tossed her mane and stared at them with her big, soft eyes as they approached the stall warily. Bess reached out a hand to her.

"Careful," Katy cautioned. "She bites."

"I know. But she's got other things to eat besides me right now," Bess laughed. She stroked the silky muzzle gently. "Oh, Blanket, you're so pretty. I always wanted a horse, but I never had the time. Mama was sick for so long, and I had to take care of her."

"What was it like where you grew up?" Katy asked.

Bess's eyes were dreamy. "Green, darling," she said wistfully. "With groves of big pecan trees and wisteria and Spanish moss hanging from the trees by the river, and fields of peanuts and soybeans. Our house was two-storied with columns, and a river-rock patio in the back. My great-grandmother was born in the front bedroom."

Katy was watching her, smiling. "Did you go to a school like I do?"

Bess shook her head. "I went to a boarding school up north. I didn't like it very much, but it was fashionable. I'd much rather have gone to a public school in town and been able to stay with my parents."

"I'm glad I go to my school," Katy said. "I like going with all my friends."

"I never had friends," Bess confided. "Except one. She died when we were in the eighth grade, and I mourned her for a long time. I . . . don't get close to people easily."

"You're close to me."

"You're different." Bess smiled. "You're very special."

The young girl hugged her. "So are you. I'm glad you're my mother."

"Darling, so am I." Bess kissed the black hair that was so like Jude's, and then reached out to stroke Blanket's nose again.

"Would you like to go riding?" Katy asked. "We've got a lot of saddle horses, and Benny's as gentle as a lamb."

Bess's eyes lit up. "Yes!"

"Come on."

Minutes later, Bess was riding the old gelding beside Katy's little buckskin mare, heading down one of the trails on the property. The air was nippy, but it felt good.

"I should have worn boots, I guess," Bess sighed, glancing down at her low-heeled walking shoes. "Not to mention jeans. This is insane, riding around in a dress. What if someone sees us?"

Katy laughed at Bess's bare legs. "Nobody will, I promise."

They rode through the woods where pines and leafless oaks and mesquite sheltered the trail, and Bess thought she'd never felt so alive. She forgot Crystal and Jude in his study; she forgot everything but the joy of being alive and gloried in the stark beauty of the landscape.

"The cattle look cold," Bess murmured, watching them as they paused beside a barbed wire fence where cactus grew in a line paralleling it. "And so am I," she added, glancing at her bare, chilly legs. "We'd better go—"

"So there you are," Jude growled, riding up on his big chestnut gelding. He looked ferocious with his hat pulled low over his eyes; his very posture spelled trouble. His eyes went to Bess's bare legs and he caught his breath. "Are you crazy?"

"Don't be mad, please, Daddy," Katy asked gently. "We just wanted to go riding, and Bess didn't want to go all the way back to the house to change."

"No, she'd rather catch pneumonia and be waited on," he growled.

"We'll go back now," Bess said quietly, turning her mount. All the sweet pleasure of the day had gone, and the excited, happy radiance of her face had paled to numb disillusionment.

"Go ahead, Katy. It's getting cold. Go play in the house," Jude said tautly.

"Yes, sir." Katy tossed an apologetic glance at the older woman and reluctantly turned back toward the barn.

Bess sat straight in the saddle and met Jude's hard eyes. "Where's Crystal?"

"Back at the house, wondering why her damned stepsister can't spare a few minutes to talk to her," he said coldly.

"You took her into your study and closed the door," she reminded him. "I assumed that meant you wanted privacy, and Katy wanted to go riding."

"Didn't you mind that I closed the door?" he asked with a watchful expression.

She had, but she wasn't going to let him know that. She shook her head. "Do what you please, Jude. I don't have the right to say anything."

He looked as if she'd hit him. She coaxed her mount forward, but his lean hand shot out and jerked the bridle, halting her.

"For God's sake, stop looking like a lost orphan," he said harshly.

"I am an orphan," she said quietly, searching his hard, shadowed eyes. "And I feel lost."

"Bess . . . damn you!"

He was out of the saddle before she could blink, reaching up to pull her down with him. And even as she looked up, stunned, his mouth went down to take total, absolute possession of hers.

"No, don't fight me," he whispered urgently when she put her hands against his chest. His mouth softened on hers, coaxing, teasing.

"I wasn't going to," she confessed. Her fingers unbuttoned his shirt, very slowly, while his mouth teased her lips and his breath rasped against them.

The shirt came open and her hands went inside it, against his warm body, spearing through cool, thick hair to find smooth, hard muscles.

His mouth grew harder with the rough caress of her hands, and she felt him shudder.

He picked her up and carried her off the trail to an open space under a huge live oak, where leaves carpeted the ground, and he laid her down.

His hands slid under her to find the zipper at her back while his mouth brushed over hers.

"I'll . . . I'll catch cold," she whispered shakily as he drew the dress down her arms and removed her bra.

"I'll keep you warm," he whispered back, and moved so that his bare chest eased down over her own bareness, his hands going under her again to bring her body up against his in a wild, hungry rhythm.

It was because of Crystal, she thought wildly, because he wanted her but couldn't forget his marriage vows, so he was venting his passion on Bess.

But even as she was thinking, her hands were twining through his black hair, dislodging his hat to give her access to it. Her body moved wildly against his.

"Please," she whimpered against his devouring mouth, her hips arching under his in helpless invitation.

"Keep that up and I'll have to," he bit off. His hands went down to her hips, grinding them into his. "Feel me?" he whispered roughly.

"I want you, too," she whispered back, her hands feverish as they tugged his shirt loose from his jeans and went under it to find the hard, smooth muscles of his back. "Oh, Jude, I want you, I want you . . . !"

"All that fire," he breathed unsteadily, lifting his head so that his mouth could reach her high, trembling breasts. "That's it, honey, that's it," he murmured when her body leaned toward him, helping him, as his lips drew slowly back and forth over soft curves, open and moist and rough in their hunger. "You're burning me alive, Bess, do you know it? I look at you and start aching. Ever since last night, when you let me see all of you and I went crazy and took you . . . I want you, right here, Bess. Right now."

He was out of control. Totally, wildly, helplessly out of control, and so was she. It was insane; Katy might come back; any one of the men might ride past . . . !

But minutes later their clothes were out of the way; it was bitterly cold but neither of them felt it, they were so hungry for each other.

He lifted her as his body overwhelmed hers in the cool silence of afternoon, and she gasped, her tiny cry merging with birdcalls from the distant meadow.

He watched her intently, his eyes blazing, cloudy with desire and recklessness, his hands hurting as they held her narrow hips to his, his heartbeat pounding as the world seemed to catch fire around them.

She heard his voice repeating her name in a feverish rush until it splintered over her, and she felt him lose control, completely lose it, while her own body tautened and tautened and finally snapped in a glorious fury.

He fought to catch his breath, his face buried in the damp hair at her throat.

"My God, we're both crazy," he said in a voice that shook. "It's damned near freezing . . ."

Her eyes were closed, her hands delicately stroking the hair at the nape of his neck while she savored this one moment of closeness, loving him with all her heart, delighting in his insanity, and her own.

He pulled himself away and rearranged his clothing, keeping his back to her while she got back into her own things. She was shaking so much she could hardly do it, and he had to zip the dress back into place for her.

"Here," he said gently, helping her into the leather jacket. "You're trembling."

She was, but it wasn't from cold. "Thank you," she said softly. She forced her eyes up to his, shy with him all at once.

His lean fingers brushed her cheek and he looked at her strangely, quietly. He bent and his mouth brushed hers in a kiss so tender that it turned her heart over.

"Every man's dream," he whispered. "A lady in public and a wildcat in bed."

She blushed, and he smiled, but it was a different kind of smile than it had been before. But only for an instant. He got to his feet and pulled her up with him.

"In the middle of the bridle path," he mused, glancing down at the disordered leaves where they'd been together. "My God."

She was pulling leaves out of her hair with trembling hands. "They'll miss us," she said shakily.

"You were the one who wanted a baby," he said, all the old sarcasm back as he stared at her. "I'm only trying to oblige."

She turned away, feeling empty all over again at the sarcasm in his voice. "Was that why?" she asked coolly. "I thought you might have gone wild over Crystal and were looking for relief."

The look on his face was a revelation. He glared at her back. "And why do you think I wouldn't look for it with Crystal?" he taunted. "She might not mind the scars in the dark, you know, and she's not inhibited, either."

Her face blazed wildly. She whirled. "Then why don't you try your luck, Rawhide Man?" she challenged with burning eyes and a cool smile. "She likes men with money."

"All the better, if she gives full value for it," he returned. He moved toward his horse. "Never mind what I said about moving into my room and sleeping with me," he said when he was mounted and his hat was back in place. "You might cramp my style."

She felt as if she might explode. But with an effort she controlled herself and got back into the saddle, gripping the reins tightly.

"It's just as well," she said. "You probably snore."

He looked as if she'd surprised him, and he

laughed unexpectedly. But before he could say anything she turned the horse and coaxed it into a canter. She couldn't handle any more sarcasm from him right now, or any more threats about Crystal. She was hurting too much.

8

~~~~~~~~~~~~~

That evening at the dinner table it was like old times for Bess as she sat quietly, picking at her food, while Crystal held court.

Her stepsister was charming, there was no doubt about that, she thought miserably as she watched her. And Jude was responding to all that blond charm like a blind man just able to see.

"Want some more corn, Bess?" Katy asked, sounding concerned.

She shook her head and even managed a convincing smile. "No, thank you, darling."

"Daddy wasn't mad at you for going riding in your dress, was he?" Katy asked under her breath.

Remembering how it had been in the woods, Bess flushed to the roots of her hair. "Uh, no," she whispered, and turned her total attention to her plate.

"Bess, I said, 'Do you remember the Cochrans?'" Crystal repeated. "I ran into them on the coast of France early in the year. Bert's in college; can you imagine?"

"That's very nice," Bess said, refusing to be drawn into the conversation. What was the use anyway? It was Jude Crystal wanted to talk to, not her.

She excused herself as soon as she could and went upstairs with Katy, while Jude watched her from his chair with an intent stare.

That night set the pattern for the next few weeks, as Crystal settled in and enlisted Jude's aid in getting her affairs in order. Apparently she'd invested some of her small inheritance from Carla and needed advice on how to play the market. It was a nice excuse, Bess thought angrily, for her to get Jude's attention as she asked him question after question about finance and investments.

For his part, Jude seemed to spend most of his time away from home on business, and if he spoke to Bess at all, it was curtly, reluctantly. He hardly ever looked at her these days, while he laughed and teased Crystal as if . . . as if she were his real wife.

"What is it like, living with Jude?" Crystal asked unexpectedly one afternoon during a rare few minutes together.

Bess glanced at her warily. "Why do you ask?"

"I'm just making conversation. Or trying to," came the exasperated reply. "Bess, I've been here just shy of a month, and we haven't really talked yet! Can't we communicate with each other? If it's because of Carla, I realize I should have shouldered more responsibility, but it's ages too late now. I can't help it that I was spoiled my whole life, can I?"

Bess looked away. She'd have loved a little of the spoiling that had always gone to Crystal, with her finely honed beauty. "Being beautiful has its advantages," she murmured.

"And its disadvantages," came the bitter reply. "Has it ever occurred to you that I never know where I am with men? Whether they want me because of me, or because of how I look? Beauty doesn't last, Bess; it's gone in such a short time. And I don't have anything to show for all mine. Not a husband or children or a future I want to look forward to."

Do you want my husband? Bess almost asked. She sighed wearily. "What about your French count?"

Crystal looked away, her features going rigid. "I hate him."

Bess almost asked what had gone wrong. She almost did, but the reticence of years made it impossible for her to go that one step toward camaraderie. She didn't know how to approach Crystal. She'd never tried.

"You'll find someone else," Bess said instead. "Would you like some coffee?"

Crystal looked at her as if she desperately

wanted to say something, but Bess's practiced coolness wasn't encouraging. She laughed shortly. "Sure, I'd love some. When is Jude coming home, by the way?"

Bess froze. "In a few days, I suppose. I'll have Aggie fix a tray," she murmured as she left the room.

"What did I say now?" Crystal asked the coffee table with a sad smile.

Bess paused in the hall to get herself back together. Why didn't Crystal just go with Jude if she wanted his company so much? He'd let her. She laughed until tears rolled down her cheeks. He'd let Crystal go anywhere with him, and at the same time, he wouldn't notice Bess if she dropped dead at his feet!

"Bess?" Crystal, hearing the unfamiliar sound of weeping, had come to the door and was standing aghast at the sight of her normally composed stepsister in tears.

Bess dried the tears with the hem of her blouse. "Sorry," she muttered, "I . . . think about Carla sometimes," she lied, letting it go at that.

"I know you miss her, darling," Crystal said gently. "I miss her too. I don't suppose I realized just how much I cared until it was too late to tell her." She reached out toward Bess, but drew back before her fingers could make contact. "Say, you don't really mind my staying, do you? Or getting Jude to help me with this financial tangle I'm in?"

"Of course not," Bess said with magnificent carelessness.

Crystal, taking the statement at face value, relaxed. "Thank goodness. I mean, I hoped you weren't jealous or anything."

Which intimated that she had reason to be. Crystal couldn't have missed the coolness between husband and wife, the pointed way they had avoided each other ever since that wild afternoon in the woods.

"I'll get the coffee," Bess said tautly.

Crystal stared after her quietly. Her lovely face was strained.

The day Jude came home Katy and Aggie had gone with Crystal to shop in San Antonio. Bess was sitting in the porch swing alone when he drove up, and her stupid heart went wild at the sight of him.

He walked up the steps as if he was bone tired, his attaché case held firmly in one lean hand.

"Isn't it a little early in the year for swinging?" he asked curtly.

She was wearing his leather jacket with jeans that, strangely enough, wouldn't fasten at the waist, and a pale yellow sweater. Her hair was in a French twist. She hadn't noticed the cold.

"I like swinging," she returned.

"Yes, I remember," he murmured, watching her closely. "Where's Crystal?"

Her face closed up and she stared out over the bleak landscape. "Gone shopping with Aggie and Katy."

His fingers contracted on the handle of the case. "Damn it, why do you do that?" he ground out.

She glanced up at him, startled. "Do what?"

"Close up like a flower whenever I come close," he said. His eyes swept over her face. "Do you think I haven't noticed? I can walk into a room when you're playing and laughing with Katy, and the color drains out of you the second you catch sight of me."

She lowered her eyes to his chest. "What do you expect me to do, run to you?"

He was rigid for an instant, his eyes narrowed. "I can't imagine you doing that," he said heavily. He set the case down on the settee and eased himself down beside Bess, lighting a cigarette on the way.

The feel of him so close was unnerving. It had been weeks since he'd touched her, since she'd been near him physically. She had to clench her hands in her lap to hide her nervousness.

"You used to spend quite a lot of time out here in the summer," he remarked, leaning back to rock the swing back into motion. "God, you were a pretty little thing, all long, tanned legs and smiles." He looked down at her assessingly. "Away from your stepsister, you blossomed. But the minute you got in the same room with her, you turned it all off. You're still doing it."

"How can I compete with someone who looks like Crystal?" she asked, as if she didn't mind. Her eyes studied her folded hands. "She could charm a dragon."

"I suppose she could. But it isn't because she's beautiful, Bess," he said. "It's because she has a bubbly personality. She reaches out."

"Is that a dig at me?" she asked curtly, glancing up.

"You don't reach out at all," he returned. "You never have. Is that why you're so eaten up with envy that you can't even stay in the same room with Crystal? Because she can communicate and you can't?"

She hated that mocking smile. She hated what he was saying. Her hand lifted toward his face without her being aware that it had moved.

He caught her wrist, and a fierce heat blazed in his green eyes, in the half-amused smile on his dark face.

"Did it hurt?" he asked curtly.

"Let go of me, you savage," she breathed furiously, her eyes glittering, her face bright with anger and frustration.

He laughed harshly as he jerked her across his lap and held her there despite her struggles. He pitched the unfinished cigarette off the edge of the porch and wrapped her tightly in his arms.

"Jude!" she protested, wriggling.

"Keep that up, honey," he breathed unsteadily in her ear, "and we'll wind up the way we were in the woods that day. Can't you feel what's happening to me?"

She was still instantly as the feel of his body got through to her. She lay quietly in his arms, aware of the sharp tang of his cologne, the clean smell of him, the warmth of his body as he held her. The hand curled around her wrist was strong and bruising. The arm at her back was just as steely. And she was awash in sensation.

He laughed softly at her embarrassment, and he released her wrist to tilt her face up to his hard eyes.

"Society girl," he growled, studying her quiet body in his arms. "Do you hate it here? Do you hate living with a man who can't recite Shakespeare and discuss the latest best seller with you?"

She gaped at him, stunned. "You're college educated," she managed.

"I took my degree in business, with a minor in economics," he reminded her. "I didn't have time for the arts."

She searched his eyes in dead silence. "I . . . I don't have much time for reading these days, and I can't . . . recite Shakespeare either."

He seemed to hesitate, and the fingers holding her chin relaxed, became caressing. "Do I know you at all?" he wondered quietly.

Her lips parted on a rush of breath. "Probably not, and what difference does it make? You wanted a mother for Katy and my share of the stock. Isn't that enough?"

"Apparently it is for you," he said, his voice cutting. He searched her eyes. "You can do without me very well, can't you, honey?"

Her eyes fell to his jutting chin. "You've been avoiding me just as hard," she said curtly.

"Do you miss me when I go away?" he challenged. He tilted her chin back up and searched her shadowy eyes. "No; hell, no, you don't."

"Why should I?" she demanded, her voice breaking.

His face hardened and a curtain fell over his darkening eyes. "I haven't been particularly kind to you, have I, Bess?" he asked after a minute. "Dragging you out here, forcing you into a marriage you didn't want, and for all the wrong reasons." His fingers touched her lips gently, softly, and he looked at her as if he'd never taken the trouble to really see her before. "Married, but not married."

"And with no way out," she said with a weary sigh.

"Yes." His voice was curt, as if he didn't like admitting that. "And up until now neither of us has made any effort to live up to our vows, have we?"

She studied him warily.

"I haven't cheated on you," he said coldly, "if that's what that searching little look was all about. The only woman I've had since we married was you."

She blushed and looked away.

His hand moved into the thickness of hair at her nape and stroked it gently. "Even that wasn't much to look back on, was it?" he asked bitterly. "Both times, I gave you hell afterwards."

"I'm sorry I was such a disappointment," she said coldly.

"You've never disappointed me," he said under his breath. "Not ever."

That brought her eyes wavering up to his and held them.

"I was like a boy with you," he breathed, grinding out the words. "I couldn't stop; I couldn't control what I felt. You . . . made me vulnerable, and I hated you for it."

Her eyes searched his, and she could hardly believe what he was admitting. "Me?"

"You." His hand stroked her throat, then moved down over the softness of the sweater, touching her hesitantly with fingers that were unexpectedly gentle. "It's been like this since I carried you out of the darkness that night you were fifteen, Bess," he said quietly, holding her eyes. "If I'd kissed you that night, we'd have gone for each other like starving wolves. We start burning up the minute we touch. You see?" he breathed, running his fingers lightly over the taut thrust of her breasts, dropping his eyes to them. "In broad daylight . . ."

Yes, she knew. Something inside her had always known how much he wanted her. But it was only desire, and that wasn't what she wanted. She wanted love.

His fingers were under the sweater now, on bare flesh, and he was watching her as they moved up.

"No bra, Bess?" he asked as his hand brushed lightly over warm, swollen flesh.

Her bras were too tight, and she hadn't had time to replace them, but she wasn't going to tell him that. She caught his wrist as the old, familiar weakness began to smother her.

"Jude, don't," she pleaded, removing his hand.

"You're mine," he said curtly. "All of you. Why shouldn't I touch you when I want to?"

Her lower lip trembled. "What's the matter, Jude, have you been missing Crystal's company so much that even I can stand in for her?" she burst out.

He froze. A black scowl darkened his face. "What did you say?"

"You want her, don't you?" she whispered. "Even if you haven't made love to her yet."

His chiseled lips parted. "Are you jealous of me?" he asked slowly.

Her eyes fell to his chin. "Let me go, please."

"No, not yet. Answer me. Are you jealous?"

Her long eyelashes swept down over her cheeks and she relaxed against him with a weary sigh. Her hand rested against the vest beneath his jacket, and he was pleasantly warm against the chill.

"Ask me why I spend time with Crystal and I'll tell you," he said over her head.

But she didn't want the answer. She didn't want to know. Impulsively, uncharacteristically, she let her head slide back onto his shoulder and curved an arm up around his neck. He looked as if she'd hit him.

She felt the advantage and took it, smiling breathlessly at the look in his glittering eyes. Her lips parted and she ran her fingers through his thick hair, carelessly dislodging the hat as she did.

The recklessness she felt was mirrored in his hard face. "Is this what you want?" he asked curtly, winding his own hand into her hair to jerk her head back. "This, Bess?"

His mouth opened on hers, forcing her lips apart,

penetrating deeply in an assault that was all wild tenderness. She arched in his arms, both hands in his hair now, her mouth answering his, demanding, needing.

The swing stopped and was still. His hands slid under the sweater again and took the warm, swollen weight of her breasts. She trembled and moaned sharply.

He lifted his dark head slowly, staring down into her hungry eyes. His thumbs edged over the taut peaks in a lazy, maddening rhythm, and all the time he looked at her, watching her helpless reaction to him.

"When are they coming back?" he asked in a voice that sounded unusually thick.

She licked her lips. "I don't know."

He bent and brushed her open mouth with his. "We could lock the bedroom door," he whispered.

"Yes." She arched again, crying out, as the pressure of his hands increased. She was unusually sore, and he drew back instantly.

"Did I hurt you?" he asked tenderly.

"I . . . I'm sore," she laughed nervously. "I don't know why."

"I'll be careful with you," he said, studying her eyes. "I'll be gentler this time, I'll take longer. I'll treat you like the virgin you were that first time, Bess."

She trembled softly in his arms as he slowly got up from the swing, cradling her against him.

"You . . . laughed the first time," she remembered shakily.

"You were wildfire in my arms, blazing with pleasure that I was giving you," he said quietly. "My God, I was so proud . . . you were a virgin, and I was making you feel that way."

She caught her breath. "I didn't know."

"I couldn't tell you." He bent and kissed her softly. "Do you really want me this time?"

Her lips parted on a wild breath. "Oh, yes, I want you," she whispered feverishly. Her arms locked around his neck and she trembled. "Jude," she moaned, arching up.

His eyes flashed as he walked into the house with her. Inside the doorway he bent, his open mouth pressing down on the high mounds of her breasts even through the fabric, and she cried out.

His heart was thundering as he walked with her toward the staircase, and she felt the same wildness they'd shared that day in the woods. He might not love her, but he wanted her. He wanted her! And, God, she wanted him!

But even as his boot touched the first step, the loud sound of a car approaching burst into the silence, and Jude cursed roughly.

"Not now," he ground out, burying his face against Bess. "Oh, God, not now!"

Her hands cradled his head and she struggled to regain her lost composure. Slowly he put her down, regret and bitterness mingling in the expression on his hard face.

She turned away, tidying her hair as best she could with her back to him.

"Bess?" he asked softly.

But before she could answer him, the door burst open and Katy and Crystal descended on them in a swirl of skirts and laughter.

"So you're finally back," Crystal laughed, following Katy's example as she ran into his arms and kissed his tanned cheek soundly. "About time, too. We've missed you, haven't we, girls?"

"Sí, we miss the sound of yelling from the study, all right," Aggie murmured with a grin as she carried packages into the living room.

"Welcome home, Daddy!" Katy laughed.

Jude, caught up in it, was laughing too, his face more relaxed than Bess had ever seen it, and she mourned the little taste of happiness she'd just lost. She turned and walked off toward the kitchen as Jude was coaxed into the living room to look at the purchases.

"Don't you want to see what they bought?" Jude asked Bess.

She stopped with her back to them, blind to the hopeful look on his face, the almost pleading one on Crystal's.

"I need some coffee. I'll make a pot, shall I?" she asked brightly, and walked away before they could question the quaver in her voice.

Bess didn't look at Jude for the rest of the night; she couldn't bear to remember how she'd tempted him. He was going to be furious about that. He always was when his fiery ardor cooled. She kept carefully out of his way until she could sneak upstairs and go to bed.

"Why didn't you go with us today?" Katy asked

as Bess tucked her into bed. "We missed you. Crystal said we should have dragged you along and made you come."

"I had things to do here, darling," Bess said with a smile. "I'm glad you had fun, though."

"I didn't. Not really," Katy admitted. She reached up and kissed Bess's cool cheek. "Crystal is fun to be with, but she just talks all the time, like she's afraid to stop, so nobody else ever gets to. You know? You listen."

Bess's eyes clouded. She kissed the young girl back. "I love you," she whispered.

Katy beamed. "I love you, too. Good night, Bess. Isn't it nice that Daddy's home?"

"Lovely, darling."

"He said he'd be up to tuck me in later. He had to talk to Crystal."

Bess nodded, turning away before Katy could see her hurt expression. "Good night, darling."

"Night, Bess, sleep well."

Back in her own room, Bess put on her flannel gown and crawled wearily into bed. She felt vaguely nauseated, and the swelling in her breasts was beginning to be uncomfortable. Something that should have happened three weeks ago hadn't, and she felt frankly nervous. It was too soon to tell, of course, but she had an odd feeling that she was carrying Jude's baby.

Her hands went unconsciously to her flat stomach. A baby. A little boy with green eyes and black hair, or a little girl who might look a lot like Katy. She smiled. Even if she lost Jude, at least she'd have the baby to love. She could give it all the warmth and adoration she longed to give to him. Except that he didn't want it. He only wanted her body, and not even that when Crystal was around.

What if Crystal did want him? She was playing her cards close, and Bess couldn't figure out why she was staying at Big Mesquite so long. Why wouldn't she go back to Oakgrove, or to France, or somewhere? But it would be impolite to ask her to leave. She laughed shortly. Jude would never let her go anyway. He . . . cared about her. He laughed with her. She hit the pillow with an angry fist. Why couldn't he laugh with Bess like that?

Even as she was silently asking the question, the door opened and Jude walked in. He was wearing his suit slacks, but only a partially unbuttoned white shirt with them. And he looked oddly tired. Worn out.

"Yes?" she asked coldly.

He laughed shortly. "So we're back to that, are we?" he asked quietly. "The mask is in place, the barriers are up. I can't get near you."

"Can't you?" she asked bitterly.

"Physically, yes," he agreed. He rammed his hands into his pockets and went to stand beside the bed, looking down at her tousled hair and flushed face with strange, lingering eyes.

"That was all you wanted, wasn't it?" she asked.

"At first." His eyes searched her face. "I must have hurt you a hell of a lot those first few weeks."

"Don't worry, Jude, I'm a survivor," she replied, lowering her eyes to the coverlet.

He sat down on the bed, tilting the mattress with his weight, and she cringed away from him.

"Oh, God, don't do that," he ground out, wincing. "Bess, I won't hurt you. I won't even touch you if you don't want it."

She relaxed a little, but she was still tense, and it showed.

"What do you want?" she asked unsteadily.

"What a question." He pulled a cigarette from his pocket and glanced at her. "Do you mind?"

She shook her head. He lit it and rose to produce an ashtray from the dresser before he sat down again. "Bess, we can't go on like this."

Cold sensations worked down her backbone. "You want a divorce?" she asked.

"No!" he burst out, scowling. "For God's sake, I told you at the beginning that it wasn't going to be a fly-by-night marriage."

"Yes, of course," she whispered.

He drew on the cigarette. "I meant, we've got to start trying. Both of us. Doing things together, living like married people. We've got to stop making our lives and Katy's a battleground."

Katy. Of course. He was worrying about Katy, as usual. She folded her hands and stared at them. "What do you suggest?"

He looked down at her. "You could start sleeping with me."

"Will your bed hold all three of us?" she asked venomously.

His eyes flashed. "I'll tell you one more time. I am not sleeping with your sister," he said coldly.

"My stepsister," she corrected.

He ran an angry hand through his thick hair. "My God, can't we even talk without arguing?"

Her face was icy, but she kept her mouth shut.

"Bess, meet me halfway," he said softly, glancing at her. "You can't know how hard this is for me. I'm painfully aware of how I've treated you. But at least make the effort, can't you?"

She watched him curiously. She wondered at this change in him. Or was it just another trick, another way to make her pay for forcing him into a marriage he didn't want?

"You don't trust me, do you?" he asked levelly.

"How can I?" she asked honestly. "Every time you let me get close, you find some nasty way of getting at me, of making me pay for what you consider your weakness."

He bent his head and smoked his cigarette quietly. "Yes," he said finally. "I suppose I do. Next to Katy, you're the only weakness I've ever discovered, society girl," he laughed bitterly.

"And you hate that," she muttered. "You hate being out of control in any way."

"Don't you?" He lifted his head, watching her. "You fought every inch of the way that first time with me, not to give in, not to let me please you. But it happened anyway, and you were angry, just as I was."

She lowered her eyes to his chest. "I was the one who paid for it," she murmured.

"Yes," he said curtly. "I hurt you. I meant to. But it backfired, in ways you can't imagine." He bent

143

over her, holding her eyes. "But all that aside, we can't go on like this. Avoiding each other, cutting at each other. We're married, Bess, for good. We've got to pick up the pieces and make a go of it."

"Then send Crystal away," she said coldly.

He lifted his chin. "Is that an ultimatum?" he asked. "Have you reached the stage where you think you can give me orders because you know I want you?"

She swallowed. "I'm not trying to do that."

"It sure as hell sounds like it." He got to his feet, glaring down at her. "I'll go halfway, lady. But I won't go the distance. When you're ready to talk sense, you know where to find me."

"Sure," she agreed. "Wherever my stepsister is."

He gave her a hot glare before he walked out the door, slamming it behind him. Bess lay there with tears running silently down her cheeks. Why hadn't she agreed to try, at least? Why were her emotions so haywire that she couldn't even talk rationally? She turned her face into the pillow. It was probably all just tension. Just tension. Her body would resume its natural rhythm in no time. She wasn't pregnant, she wasn't! It was all just her own imagination.

As the days passed, Jude invited her to go places with him: into town to buy wire, on brief trips to neighboring ranches, to social affairs. And she turned down every invitation abruptly and without explanation.

"My God, Bess, won't you even try?" he growled one night in exasperation.

"I am trying. To be left alone," she returned.

He sighed wearily, watching her in an increasingly familiar way, one that turned her weak. "One day I'm going to take the choice right out of your hands, honey," he said in a menacingly soft tone. "I'm going to carry you up to my bed and love you out of your mind. Then we'll talk."

She flushed and got up out of her chair. "About what? About how you hate wanting me?" she asked. "Well, I don't want you, Jude. Not anymore."

He made a sudden move toward her, and she backed up against the door, wide-eyed and frightened.

He scowled darkly at that look and hesitated. "I could make you beg," he said harshly.

Didn't she know it. Her eyes closed. "What would be the point?" she asked gently. "I haven't made any trouble lately, have I? I've been polite and sweet to Crystal, and you and I have put on a grand front. Katy thinks everything is just fine."

He sighed wearily. "Bess, do you hate me?" he asked quietly.

She studied his face, noticing how tired and worn he looked, how sad. "No," she said. "I don't hate you."

He moved toward her slowly. "We could sleep together," he said. "No sex. Just sleep. We could try to get used to each other."

But she couldn't bear that. Especially now. Because she was beginning to lose her breakfast each morning, and Jude wasn't stupid. He'd know.

She swallowed. "I . . . like sleeping alone," she whispered.

"That's the whole damned problem with our marriage," he said curtly. "You like doing everything alone!"

"Well, I didn't drag you out here and force you to marry me!" she burst out, tears welling up in her eyes.

He reached out and dragged her into his arms, holding her close, rocking her like a child. "Hush, honey," he whispered. "Hush, now, don't cry. Don't. Please don't." His hand soothed her cheek, her hair. His lips touched her forehead, her cheeks, the corner of her tear-washed mouth. "Don't cry, honey, I can't stand it."

He was so tender. Tender in a way he never had been before, and she reacted to it helplessly, letting him dry her tears with his handkerchief.

"So trusting," he breathed, studying her eyes. "You used to look at me like that once. In the very beginning. And I cut you like a whip, didn't I?"

She dropped her eyes to his chest. "You didn't want to marry me. I understood."

His hands caught her shoulders and held them bruisingly tight. "I didn't want to marry anyone. But I wanted you so damned much. I'd wanted you for years. And once I had you, all I could think about was having you again." He leaned his forehead against hers with a weary sigh. "Bess, I get up wanting you in the morning and I go to bed wanting you at night. Isn't that revenge enough for you?"

It was. Oh, yes, it was. But she didn't think she could bear to be intimate with him again when he didn't love her.

"I'm so tired, Jude," she whispered. "I need to sleep."

He drew away, studying her. "You really don't want me anymore?" he asked quietly.

Gritting her teeth, she slowly shook her head.

He let her go finally with a rough laugh and turned away. "I'm not even surprised. Women haven't made a habit of wanting me."

He was at the door when she remembered Elise and the scars and all the torment he'd sustained at the hands of women who didn't want him.

"Jude!" she cried.

But he wouldn't look at her. "Go to sleep, Bess. I won't bother you again."

And with that mocking remark, he went out and closed the door between them.

9

The next morning Crystal was at the breakfast table when Bess got there, sitting next to Jude and apparently flirting for all she was worth.

"There you are, finally," Crystal chided. "I thought you were going to spend the day in bed."

Actually, she'd been in the bathroom, not in bed, feeling sicker than usual first thing in the morning. But it wouldn't do to let that out, so she smiled instead.

"I was sleepy," she told her stepsister. "Hi, Katy," she added, winking at the young girl. Jude, she ignored.

"Crystal wants to go and see the Alamo this morning," he said, forcing her to look at him.

"You'll have fun, I'm sure," she replied coolly.

"You and Katy are coming too," he continued, finishing his eggs.

"No, I'm not," Bess replied. "I don't feel like hiking around downtown."

His eyes narrowed. "I said, you're coming."

"Now, Bess, don't spoil the day for the rest of us," Crystal coaxed, and shook back her glorious hair. "You were telling Katy the other day that you wanted to see it. Why not today?"

Bess could have told her stepsister why not, but she bit her tongue and sipped her coffee instead. "All right," she said finally.

"You'll like it, honest you will," Katy promised. "You and I will go around the grounds and I'll show you this neat old squirrel who poses for pictures."

"She isn't kidding," Jude said with a quiet smile. "He's an old squirrel, and he actually will stand still when he's photographed."

"Have you taken his photo, Jude?" Crystal asked.

"No, but my office is near the Alamo grounds. Sometimes, in the spring, I walk around there at lunchtime on my way to a restaurant."

Bess studied his hard face as he smiled back at Crystal, and she wished that he'd smile at her like that. But it wasn't good to live in a dream world, she told herself, and finished her breakfast.

The Alamo Plaza was located near the historic Menger Hotel, and Bess was surprised by the immensity of its grounds, which included paved walkways and benches and tables as well as buildings, all dedicated to the preservation of the old mission's history.

The second stone church of Mission San Antonio de Valero stood with ancient dignity, flanked by gates on either side, which led to the rest of the compound. Bess touched the scarred stone with fingers that trembled as she felt the bravery and torment of the 180-odd men who had died there one cold March day in 1836. Her eyes moved up and down it with quiet awe as she tried to imagine what it would have been like to face certain death at the hands of Santa Anna's overwhelming Mexican forces.

"Six of the men who died here were Georgians, including Bowie, though some people say he was actually from Kentucky," Jude told her, moving to her side.

She glanced up. "Really?"

"Some were from Ireland and England and Germany. Travis was from South Carolina, Crockett from Tennessee." His own lean hand touched the surface of the building. "They left us quite a legacy. It takes a special kind of courage to face death in the way they faced it."

"They were special men," she murmured.

"And used to seeing death," he added. "They lived in hard times, without any of the luxuries we take for granted today. They were veteran fighters for the most part."

"I've read several books about the siege," she mentioned. "Most of them disagree on how many men died here," she added.

"There were eyewitness accounts by those who survived it," he reminded her. "They give the best chronology. Come here."

He led her inside and pointed out the room where the powder and shot had been kept and where Jim Bowie had lain on his cot when the enemy broke in. Another large room was railed off with wrought iron, and flags were placed inside.

"Some of that graffiti on the wall is very old," he explained while she tried to decipher the aged scribbling.

There were paintings on the wall depicting the two-hour battle when Mexican troops had overrun the walls, and weapons under glass cases, along with other memorabilia. The stone floor, he added, was a later addition. The floor of the Alamo had been dirt at the time of the actual battle.

She stood by the rear exit and shivered, looking up at the ceiling, listening silently to the echo as a tourguide outlined the days of the siege and the final battle.

"Cold?" Jude asked gently.

She shook her head. "It's just . . ." She looked at him helplessly. "I've read about the Alamo, you know, but actually being here . . . it's very different. It's more than pages in a book now. I feel strange."

He slid an arm around her and drew her close against his side. "They knew what they were doing," he said, glancing around. "And why they were doing it. It was what happened here, and at Goliad, that united Texans into the force that won victory with Sam Houston at San Jacinto. And that led to Texas independence and statehood. All because a handful of men wouldn't raise a white flag." He glanced down at her. "Even the women had spirit."

She looked up at him and smiled slowly, softly. Her dark eyes searched his pale green ones. "Did they?"

His breath came quickly. His jaw tautened. "Bess—"

"There you are," Crystal interrupted. "Come on, you two. Let's go see the souvenirs."

There was a huge live oak outside the Alamo, its limbs held aloft with chains, just in front of the ruins of the Long Barracks, where the last stand had been made. Jude still had his arm around Bess and she pressed closer unconsciously as she stared at the darkened doorways.

"I don't want to go in there," she said quietly.

"Me, neither," Katy said firmly. "Let's go see the squirrel, please."

Crystal only shrugged. "I think I'd rather go to the museum. Have they got turquoise in the museum shop? I love turquoise."

She led the way, and Bess didn't argue about going there first. She was in heaven so close to Jude, and he didn't seem in the least anxious to let her go, either.

But once they were inside, there was so much to see that the two of them became separated. Bess wandered around looking at the manuscripts and coins and historical portraits and guns displayed in the building, while Crystal and Katy hung around the gemstones and souvenirs.

Crystal talked Jude into buying her a ridiculously expensive turquoise bracelet. Katy he bought a "coonskin" cap.

"What do you want, Mrs. Langston?" he asked Bess, his eyes twinkling, and she realized suddenly that he was happy, and that she hadn't seen him that way before.

Her lips parted, and she tried to think. What would she like if she had only one tiny memento of their time together? Something . . .

"I'd like . . . I'd like a ring," she said.

His face brightened, and his eyes glimmered down at her. "A ring?"

"A gemstone one."

He led her over to the counter and let her look. She picked out a silver band with inlaid turquoise which, when the saleslady took it out of the glass case, fit her ring finger exactly. She put her simple gold wedding band on after it and stared at it lovingly.

Jude paid for it—it wasn't a tenth as expensive as Crystal's—with a curious frown.

"Is that all you want?" he asked, as Crystal and Bess went out the door toward the wishing well in the courtyard.

"Yes," she said, staring at the new ring. "Thank you, Jude."

"You could have had a silver wedding band," he said. "I . . . didn't think to ask you."

"It didn't matter," she said quietly. "I like this

ring. It's simple, but it has a grace and dignity that I don't associate with diamonds."

"You're a strange lady."

"What does that make you?" she asked, glancing up. "You married me."

"Yes," he said absently, watching her. "I married you."

"But not out of choice." She dropped her eyes.

"About the marriage, Bess . . . ," he began slowly.

"Don't bother," she said quickly. "We've been over it and over it, and nothing ever changes. We only argue."

"We might not, if you'd meet me halfway. You might run toward me for a change, instead of from me."

"It's safer running from you," she said sharply, glaring up at him. "It hurts less!"

His face paled and he looked bitter. "I realize I haven't been particularly kind to you. In case it's escaped your notice, I'm trying damned hard not to hurt you these days, but you're determined not to make it easy for me."

She gaped at him. "Are you trying? I wouldn't call hanging around Crystal's neck trying very damned hard!"

"Are you jealous? Answer me this time."

She turned away. "I am not. And if I were, I'd die before I'd let you know it. I don't give away troop movements to the enemy, Mr. Langston," she added, glaring back at him.

"Am I the enemy these days?" he asked.

"What do you think?"

He sighed heavily. "I try not to think anymore, Bess."

Katy came running back toward them, her eyes aglow. "It's the squirrel. Hurry, Bess, there's a man feeding him nuts!"

The man was still feeding him nuts when Bess arrived, and the grizzled old squirrel was taking them right from his hand.

"Ain't he a character?" the elderly man chuckled as the rodent took the nut from his fingers. "Sure is a hit with the tourists. They can't get over how tame he is."

"I wish I had my camera," Bess said enthusiastically. "What a picture he'd make."

Obviously another tourist felt the same way, because she moved forward with a 35-mm camera and clicked away.

Bess had thought that everyone would want to go home after their excursion, but they wound around through the downtown area, through La Villita with its arts and crafts, and on to the Paseo del Rio, the River Walk. They saw the Arneson River Theatre, with its seats carved into the bank, and the dozens of restaurants and pubs along the way where in the spring and summer tourists could sit outside and watch the river run. Bess sighed as she strolled alongside it, wishing that the weather were warm and she could sit and daydream by its banks. She was already getting tired, feeling her pregnancy in a new way.

Jude caught her arm. "Want to rest a few minutes?" he asked gently.

She looked up, surprised by his courtesy. "Yes, I would," she confessed.

He smiled at her. "Just a few more feet and up the steps."

He led them into a restaurant overlooking the river, the same one in which they'd once argued so fiercely. They were seated and handed long, impressive menus by a courteous waiter. Bess was feeling strangely hungry, so she ordered a prime rib.

Jude watched her, his eyes oddly protective, while Crystal, as usual, kept up an animated flow of conversation. She continued it all through the meal, but when they started back toward Joske's, near which they had parked the car, it was Bess's arm Jude took, not Crystal's. It was as if he were afraid she might get away from him.

When they got back to the house Bess went immediately to her room and lay down. She felt tired to the bone, and a little nauseated. But most of all, she was confused. Confused as to what Jude wanted of her . . . what she wanted herself.

10

Bess fell asleep and when she woke again it was dark outside. She rolled over onto her back, feeling oddly cool, and suddenly realized that she was wearing a nightgown. She blinked, staring at the ceiling. Had she taken time to put it on?

The door opened while she was getting oriented again, and Jude came in with a tray.

"Awake at last," he murmured, putting it down on the bedside table. "Aggie thought you needed feeding."

She propped herself up against the pillows with a soft smile. "I'm starved," she admitted. Shyly she glanced at him. "Did you put this on me?" she asked, picking at the soft white lacy gown.

"You were sound asleep in your jeans and shirt,"

he remarked, studying her. "I thought you'd be more comfortable this way."

"I am. Thank you."

"Here," he said, offering her a spoonful of Aggie's special chicken and broccoli crepe.

She took it, savoring the creamy taste, and smiled. "Delicious!" She started to take the spoon from him, but he ignored her and kept on until he'd fed her every bite.

"Want some dessert?" he asked. "Aggie made an apple pie."

She shook her head. "I couldn't eat another bite!"

"You look as if you've gained a little weight," he murmured as he put the plate aside. "Your jeans weren't buttoned. Only zipped."

She kept her nerve, but barely. "I've been eating more lately," she lied. "Besides, what do you care if I gain weight? You never notice."

His head turned back, and against his thick black lashes his eyes were unusually green. "I notice everything about you," he said quietly. "Everything."

"Do you?" She dropped her eyes to his shirt. "But you notice Crystal more."

His lean hand moved to her cheek, turning her face toward his. "Crystal knows how to flirt, honey. You've never bothered to learn."

"Meaning I should learn from her?" Her eyes glared accusingly at him. "What could she possibly teach me except how to be promiscuous?"

"You do hate her, don't you?" he asked with

narrowing eyes. "Is it really because she sleeps around? Or because you're jealous of her success with men?"

"Damn you!"

His eyes searched hers. "How unladylike, Mrs. Langston," he said with amusement. "You know, you've lost a lot of your starch since you've been here. You're still a lady, but you're more human."

"Look who's talking about being human," she threw back. "What would you know about that?"

"Is that a question or a dare?" he murmured. He leaned down, resting his weight on his hands on either side of her. "I asked you once to sleep with me and you turned me down. Suppose I take the choice away from you, the way I did before?"

She felt herself panic. She was all too vulnerable to him. She still needed time to straighten out her feelings about their marriage.

"Please don't," she whispered.

He looked calculating, not angry or particularly disappointed. "If I promised to be very gentle?" he whispered, searching her eyes quietly. "Not to hurt?"

She could feel herself weakening, because the way he was looking at her was different from any way he'd looked at her before. She could hardly breathe for the wild beating of her heart. But she couldn't do what he wanted her to do. Not yet.

She lowered her eyes. "I . . . don't feel that way anymore, I told you last night," she bit off.

"You told me. I just didn't quite believe you." He stood up, and his look was unnerving. "Is it just me, or are you frozen clean through? Damn it, you wanted me when we married."

"Yes, I did," she said. "And you threw it in my face until I choked on it!"

He turned away. "I suppose I did," he said wearily. He ran a hand through his hair. "But on the front porch, when you were sitting in the swing . . . and that hasn't been so long ago, lady."

She avoided his accusing gaze. "That was then. This is now."

"What's changed?"

"You!" she burst out, glaring at him. "I don't know what to make of you. And I just don't dare trust what you say. First you force me into marrying you, but you don't want anything to do with me. Then you want me in bed, but you go out of your way to hurt me. Now you say you want to make the marriage work. Sometimes I think you enjoy torturing me!"

"Is that what it seems like?" He moved back to the bed with a weary sigh. "Bess, must we fight? I'll be the first to admit that I've given you plenty of reason not to trust me. But there has to be a common ground."

"Does there?" She stared at the coverlet blankly.

He tilted her chin up. "You look different lately," he murmured, changing the subject. "Your face is rounder; your breasts are bigger." His eyes went down to them and she flushed.

"Thank you for bringing up my supper," she said.

"Thank you and good night?" he asked. He

stood up and laughed curtly. "I had you in the palm of my hand once upon a time, Bess. What a pity that I was too damned stupid to realize what I was holding until it was too late." He picked up the tray. "Get some rest, honey. Maybe we'll eventually be able to sort things out."

"Is Crystal still up?" she asked as he started toward the door.

He glanced back at her, looking strangely pleased. "Yes, as a matter of fact, she is. Jealous, honey?"

She was getting tired of having him ask that. Her eyes flashed wildly. "Go away! I hate men. I hate you. I hate Crystal. I hate the whole world!"

He only laughed, moving gracefully toward the door. "When you get tired of brooding, come and get me. You might discover that it's easier than you think."

But Bess only half heard him. She was too busy trying not to cry. How could he, how could he!

She tossed and turned all night, her mind overwhelmed with images of Crystal with Jude, dark and light, in bed together. She'd kill him. She'd kill Crystal. She'd leave and go home to Georgia. She'd do something! But when she awoke, worn out and feeling deathly ill, revenge was the last thought in her mind.

She glanced at the clock and realized that it was already past time for church and she'd never make it before services were over. With a weary sigh, she pulled on a loose gray dress and brushed her hair, leaving it long.

She went downstairs, but the house was oddly quiet. There was a muffled sound in the den, where the door was ajar.

Her hand reached out and pushed the door gently open. Her face went paper white. Crystal was wrapped tight in Jude's arms and they were kissing. Bess stood there gaping at them, her whole life flashing in front of her, hating them, hating them!

At that moment Jude lifted his head, laughing, and saw Bess. The look on his face would have been, in another time and place, utterly comical. But to Bess, whose whole world had just gone down in ashes, it was only confirmation of her worst suspicions.

Crystal stared at her with her mouth open. "Now, Bess," she began hesitantly. "Darling, let me . . ."

"It isn't what you think," Jude added slowly, his own face oddly pale under his deep tan.

"Of course not," Bess said. Her lower lip trembled and all the years of control, all the years of cool acceptance went flaming up in the grip of the worst fury she'd ever felt.

"Damn you," she threw at Crystal, her brown eyes blazing, her face lined with anger, "you tramp! It isn't enough that you spent the past ten years taking everything of mine you could lay your hands on, or that you went flying off to Europe and left me alone to take care of Mother all those long years. No, you had to come out here and make a grab for my family."

Crystal was slowly turning pale herself. "Bess, wait—"

"Wait, hell!" she shot back. Her fists clenched by her sides. "All the years I dated, you stole every single beau I had. You coaxed Carla into giving you my grandmother's jewels, the heirlooms I would have passed to my children, and you hocked them to get money! You even had the gall to question the will that left Oakgrove to me. Oakgrove, for God's sake, that had been in my family for a hundred years! And now you want Jude."

"Darling, Bess, please . . . !" Crystal pleaded, moving toward her.

But Bess backed away, hating them both. She tore the wedding bands from her hand—the gold one Jude had reluctantly slid onto her finger, and the silver one he'd bought her at the Alamo.

"You might as well have it all," she said harshly, and flung the rings at Crystal. "All of it! Finally, this time, you've taken something I didn't want to begin with!"

Jude looked as if she'd slapped him. He didn't even move.

"I'm going home," Bess wept, brushing wildly at the tears on her cheeks. "If I have to walk every step of the way. And I never want to see either of you, ever again!"

Blindly she turned and rushed out of the study, deaf to Crystal's harsh plea. Without any particular course in mind, she threw open the front door and ran for the steps. But, blinded by her own tears, she didn't see the first one. She lost her footing and tumbled headfirst down the long wooden row of steps, feeling at first a sudden, sharp pain, and then a quiet black oblivion.

The dreams were wild and strange. She was drowning as she reached out toward Jude, but he was dancing with Crystal, and she couldn't make him hear her. She was drowning, drowning . . .

"Wake up now, wake up, that's it," came a slow, soothing voice.

She opened her heavy eyelids and looked up into a round face with glasses behind an optical tool with a light in its center.

"Hello," she murmured drowsily.

"Hello, yourself," he murmured back. He looked in her other eye and stood up. "Well, that doesn't look too bad. You were lucky."

She swallowed, looking around the room. It was empty except for a nurse hovering in the background. "The baby?" she whispered, frightened as she remembered the long fall. Her eyes looked up into his for reassurance. "What about my baby?"

He frowned. "Are you pregnant?"

"Yes, I think so," she whispered unsteadily, and proceeded to tell him about her symptoms.

He examined her again, very carefully, and ordered tests. "You'll need to stay overnight," he said. "I don't think you've done any damage, but we'll have to make sure." He patted her on the shoulder. "Don't worry, now. We'll take good care of you."

"Doctor, please, if my husband and family are

out there, don't tell them about the baby just yet," she asked pleadingly.

He lifted an eyebrow and grinned. "Don't steal your thunder, huh? Okay. But if I don't let that husband of yours in here pretty quick, I won't have any staff left. He's been chewing them out ever since he brought you in here. I'll get him."

Not Jude, she wanted to say. Not now, please, when I'm too weak to fight. But that would have sounded strange, and she wasn't up to explanations, either.

She closed her eyes, and when she opened them Jude was standing over her, white as paste and with eyes that frightened her.

"How do you feel?" he asked tautly.

She licked her dry lips and tried to breathe normally. They'd given her something for the pain and she was already feeling foggy.

"I feel sort of numb," she whispered.

He reached down and touched her hand very lightly, as if he expected her to jerk away from him, and she saw that her wedding bands had been replaced on it. "He said you weren't hurt. Why are they keeping you?" he asked in an odd tone.

"Just . . . to do some . . . tests," she said. "I'm okay."

His fingers curled around hers and tightened. His jaw clenched. "Oh, God, honey . . . ," he ground out, closing his eyes. "Bess!"

He sounded terrified. If only she weren't so sleepy. She tried to get her hand away from his because she wanted to reach up and touch him.

But he misunderstood the weak gesture and moved away.

"Shall I stay with you?" he asked tautly.

But she was already fading out and she didn't hear him. The pain was going away. . . .

When she came to again it was dark. Very dark, and quiet. She opened her eyes just in time to see Crystal come in the door with a Coca-Cola in one hand.

Her eyes went cold and she started to speak, but Crystal moved toward the bed quickly.

"Please, don't get upset," Crystal pleaded gently, her face a mask of pure anguish. "Please, Bess. They'll make me leave, and I've got to stay with you. I promised Jude I wouldn't leave you alone for a second."

She lay back on the pillows with a bitter sigh and closed her eyes. Maybe she could pretend she wasn't conscious.

"Please listen," Crystal begged softly. "Please. Then if you want me to go, I'll call a nurse or somebody to stay with you instead of me. All right?"

"I can't go anywhere," Bess said weakly, turning her head away.

"No, you can't." Crystal sat down by the bed, putting her soft drink on the elevated tray nearby. "What you saw . . . I swear to God, it wasn't anything more than gratitude. Despite what you seem to think, I didn't come here to steal your husband. As if I could," she laughed. "Jude doesn't want me."

166

Bess stared at the wall, wishing her stepsister would just go away.

"I got a phone call this morning from Jacques, my Frenchman," she said softly. "He wants to marry me, Bess. Can you imagine? He actually wants to marry me!"

That drew Bess's attention for the first time. She turned her head on the pillow and stared at Crystal.

"I didn't dream that being away would make him miss me that much," Crystal continued quietly. "Even though Jude told me that if Jacques cared at all, it would happen. I wanted to leave weeks ago, but he asked me to stay. I thought maybe he was spending time with me to try and make you jealous. And I played up to him a little, to see if I could help." She smiled sadly. "But all I did was make things worse. Darling, you're so . . . withdrawn. You won't let any of us near enough to hurt you. I suppose I even understand." She reached out hesitantly and touched her stepsister's arm. "I've been pretty callous at times, haven't I? I knew you didn't want me here. But I kept telling myself that if I tried a little harder I might be able to reach you. I just wanted someone to talk to, Bess," she finished. "I had no one else, only you."

Bess's eyes felt wet. "Why didn't you tell me?" she burst out.

Crystal stared at her lap. "I didn't know how. It's all bluff with me, Bess. I laugh and tease and pretend that I'm always on a high. But I can't stop acting and be myself. Especially with the people who matter."

"Like Jacques?"

She nodded, smiling. "You see, he thought there was nothing under the fluff. He thought I was a shallow little flirt with no real feelings. He told me so. I came here hurting, but I hid it so well that nobody knew. Except Jude," she added quietly. "I suppose he's been hurt so much that he knew the signs."

Bess closed her eyes. She couldn't bear to think about that.

"Please don't hate me," Crystal said unsteadily. "I was thanking him in the only way I could. I wouldn't have hurt you for the world."

Bess reached out and gently touched Crystal's hand. "I'm sorry I didn't understand," she said softly. "I'm sorry for the things I said. . . ."

"You had every right," Crystal returned. The hurt faded out of her eyes and she smiled. "Wow, what a temper!"

Bess laughed self-consciously. "I never knew I had one, except when Jude baited me."

"Poor old guy," she murmured. "He's paid today for sins he hasn't even bothered to commit."

Bess searched her stepsister's eyes. "Is he here?"

"All day long," came the quiet reply. "Up until just a few minutes ago. I made him go get something to eat. He's sick about what happened. He feels responsible."

That was like Jude, to bear the brunt of responsibility for whatever happened to his possessions. Wasn't that what she was?

She smiled bitterly. "Well, I'm all right now. He can go home and . . ."

"And do what?" Crystal asked quietly. "Bess, that man loves you. I've never seen a man suffer the way he did when you fell down those steps. I had to call the ambulance; he wouldn't leave you even that long. And when the ambulance attendants came, they had to work around him because he wouldn't let go. He was terrified. Thank God Katy wasn't home when it happened."

"Katy!" Bess tried to sit up, but she held her head as it began to throb. She lay back down. "Poor Katy, have you called her?"

"Hours ago," Crystal said. "She and Aggie are at the house."

"I feel like such a fool," Bess moaned. "All this, because I was eaten up with jealousy and couldn't admit it." Her eyes searched Crystal's. "Can you forgive me?"

"If you can forgive me," came the soft reply. "Oh, Bess, don't you know that I'd never be able to compete with you? You're so gentle and caring, so giving with the people you do open up to. You're warm and generous, and you have a poise and sophistication I'll never have in a million years. Beauty fades. But character never does."

Bess held out her arms, crying as she embraced her stepsister.

"Are you really okay?" Crystal asked as she drew back, frowning.

Bess nodded. "Just a little whacked and bruised. But I'll be fine, now. Really I will."

"That's good. Because I have to catch a plane to France in the morning, before a certain count changes his mind about that emerald engagement ring he promised me." Crystal grinned. "Will you mind?"

"Not if I can come to the wedding," she replied, amazed at the ease with which they conversed now.

Crystal grinned. "You'll get the first invitation. Jude can bring you."

The smile faded. "Yes."

Crystal squeezed her hand. "Give him a chance," she said. "He hasn't had an easy time of it either."

"He takes his responsibilities seriously," Bess agreed tiredly.

"You're more than that to him, darling. If you'd seen him the way I did, you'd realize that. Now get some rest. I'll sit here and sip my Coke and in the morning you'll be all better. Okay?"

"Okay." She smiled, clutching Crystal's slender hand as she drifted off to sleep peacefully for the first time.

When she opened her eyes again, the doctor was there and Crystal was blowing her a kiss from the doorway.

"I feel like Santa Claus," Dr. Barnes said with a grin after Crystal had left. "Which do you want, a boy or a girl?"

"I'm really pregnant?" she asked, rising.

"You're really pregnant," he chuckled. "Not bad news, I gather?"

"Oh, gosh," she breathed. She lay back down, grinning like a child. "Oh, gosh." Her hands went to her stomach and all of a sudden she felt wonderful.

"No sense talking to you any more tonight, I can see that," he murmured after he checked her over. "Baby's fine. So are you. I may let you out of here tomorrow; we'll see in the morning. Sleep tight!"

But she only smiled. What a wonderful, sweet secret. She closed her eyes and carried it off into the dark with her.

11

⋘⋙

Sunlight streamed in through the blinds and she moved restlessly. She felt bruised from head to toe, aching and miserable.

Her eyes opened and Jude was sitting rigidly in a chair by the bed. His eyes were bloodshot, staring straight ahead in a face like rawhide. His black hair was disheveled, and the pale blue silk shirt he was wearing with a blazer and dark slacks looked rumpled. It was unbuttoned halfway down, displaying bronzed muscles and curling dark hair, and she remembered with a shock of pleasure how it had felt to touch him there.

"Jude?" she whispered.

He sat up, his face alert, his eyes probing. "How are you?" he asked tautly.

"A little bruised," she said, avoiding that probing stare. "Where's Crystal?"

"On her way to Paris. She said she'd phone you tonight."

"Yes, I'd like that."

He studied her wan face. "She said you talked last night."

She nodded. Her eyes glanced off his. "Crystal told me why she was kissing you. I'm sorry for the accusations I made," she said gruffly.

He caught her hand and pressed the palm hotly to his mouth, his eyes closing as he kissed the soft flesh hungrily. "Shut up, will you?" he asked on a harsh laugh. "My God, when I saw you pitch down those steps I wanted to put a gun to my temple!"

"It wasn't your fault," she managed shakily.

"The hell it wasn't." He kissed her palm again before he laid it back gently on the bed. He got to his feet, stretching as he went to the window and opened the blinds. "The doctor said you could go home today."

"I'd like that."

"If you feel like it," he emphasized. "I don't want you taking chances."

"I'm okay," she said, touched by the concern in his voice.

He turned from the window and moved back to the bed. "Bess," he said, oddly hesitant as he looked down at her, "Aggie said you were losing your breakfast lately."

She looked up at him through her lashes and her heart ran wild. "Did she?"

He sat beside her, touching her hand, feeling the rings that were back in place. His hand moved to the warm swell of her stomach and lingered there, pressing tenderly. "Are you going to give me a baby, honey?" he asked, looking into her eyes with a warm, questioning glance.

It was the wording as much as the deep velvet of his voice that made her flush with warmth. She hesitated a second, searching his hard face. Her fingers touched his tentatively. "Yes, I am," she said after a minute.

He studied her body in the shapeless gown, learning the new contours of her waistline and stomach, and he smiled gently. But when he looked up, the smile faded. "Couldn't you tell me?"

Her fingers lifted and brushed softly across the dark skin and hair on the back of that long-fingered hand. Amazingly, it trembled. "I was afraid," she said softly.

"Of me?" he asked, anguished.

"No!" She looked up, feeling his fingers lock into hers and draw them onto his broad, powerful thigh. "Of making you feel more tied than you already were. I . . . I thought you wanted Crystal, Jude."

"And I thought you didn't want me," he said quietly. "You even told me you didn't."

"Because I wasn't sure of you," she replied. Her eyes fell to their locked hands. "I never have been. You're so self-sufficient, so controlled. I never know what you're thinking or feeling."

"That makes two of us." His fingers contracted. "I put the rings back on, did you notice?"

"Yes. Thank you. I didn't mean half of what I said. My emotions seem to have gone haywire lately."

His hand freed hers and moved, lightly, reverently, over the soft swell of her stomach. "Does he move yet?" he whispered.

She smiled shyly. "It's too soon. You really don't mind?"

He smiled back. "No. I told you at the very beginning that I'd like to have a baby with you, didn't I?"

"You made some pretty horrible remarks about that," she reminded him.

"Self-defense, Bess," he said quietly. "I told you once that you made me lose control. I'd put a wall between myself and the world, and here you came, knocking out bricks. I didn't understand that at the time, and I liked it even less. So I fought back, with the only weapons I had."

"And now?"

"Now, I'm sorry I didn't start off better with you," he said. "I kept Crystal here thinking that her Frenchman might miss her and come looking. And," he admitted, "that she might make you a little jealous. If I'd realized how tragic the consequences could have been, I'd have sent her packing the first day. If you'd been badly hurt or lost the baby, I couldn't have lived with it."

"You didn't know I was going to start screaming over an innocent kiss," she said ruefully.

"It was that, for what it's worth. She was so excited about being reunited with her man that she had to share it. I'm sorry that I let her, now." He searched her face. "And she was kissing me, not the reverse. I . . . don't want other women, Bess. Only you."

Her face glowed at his remark, blossomed. His eyes made slow, sensuous love to hers in the silence that followed, and the lean hand across her stomach began to move in whisper soft patterns. His head bent toward her; his eyes glittered with possession. The silence magnified the sound of her unsteady breathing. The moment blazed with promise. His hand started to slide up toward one swollen breast, and her body lifted ardently to meet its ascent while her lips opened to welcome his. His breath caught as his mouth halted, poised just above hers.

At that moment, Dr. Barnes walked in, all smiles, and flopped into a chair to discuss the baby. Ignoring the flustered embarrassment of the parents-to-be, he gave them the name of a good obstetrician, congratulated Jude, and gave Bess some high-powered prenatal vitamins to take.

"Eat properly from now on," Dr. Barnes added. "You're much too thin."

"She'll eat if I have to force-feed her," Jude said arrogantly.

She glared at him, and Dr. Barnes laughed. "Good man," the doctor chuckled. "You get in touch with this obstetrician, young lady, and make an appointment. Prenatal care is important. If you're interested in natural childbirth, by the way, the hospital has classes. Your obstetrician can tell you more about that."

"I'd like that," Bess said.

"So would I," Jude murmured surprisingly, glancing at her. "We'll take them together."

She had to hide her eyes to keep him from seeing the shock of pleasure the words had given her. After the doctor left, the rest of the morning passed in a wild haze, and before she knew it Jude had checked her out and she was home again.

From the minute she walked in the door of Big Mesquite, and Katy hugged and hugged her, she felt different. And things *were* different. Jude strutted around like a proud father, watching her hawklike as if he was constantly searching for something in her expression. And as if his close scrutiny weren't surprise enough, when the women got ready for church the following Sunday, they found Jude in a gray suit waiting for them downstairs.

"You're going to church with us?" Bess asked, astonished.

He glared at her. "Is there anything wrong with a man taking his family to church?"

"No, of course not," she stammered.

"Then shut up and let's go, before you make us late," he said, herding the three of them out the door.

Katy giggled, but she didn't let her father hear her, and Aggie just shook her head with wonder.

The Methodist minister at the church where they attended services looked as if he might faint when he saw Jude sitting in one of the front pews with his family. But he recovered quickly and grinned from ear to ear.

Bess, sitting beside her handsome husband, felt on top of the world. It was a mark of how far they'd come, for Jude to willingly walk into a house of worship. The cold, hard man she'd married so many long months ago wouldn't have been caught dead in one.

He struggled through the songs as if he hadn't sung in a long time, but he had a rich baritone and Bess thought he sounded wonderful. She smiled up at him mischievously. He turned his head, catching it, and grinned back. It was a small invitation, but more than enough for Bess, who was starving for something even closer than the friendly relationship they had shared since her return from the hospital.

That night, Bess tucked Katy into bed and didn't linger as she usually did. Pleading a headache, she excused herself, thinking she hadn't really lied to Katy. Jude did tend to be one, on occasion.

She heard water running as she entered the sanctuary of his bedroom, and had to force her nervous legs to carry her inside it. She locked the door behind her.

Jude's bedroom had dark Mediterranean furniture, with brown and cream accessories and a huge bed. She flushed as she looked at it, because it loomed large in her plans for the rest of the evening. She tugged the powder blue satin robe she wore closer around her nudity and walked purposefully into the adjoining brown and cream bathroom.

He was in the shower, with the glass door closed, just rinsing his hair. She sat down on the stool by the door and watched with rising excitement, because the textured glass was almost transparent and she was getting fascinating glimpses of brown skin and thick black hair that arrowed down chest and stomach and thighs.

Seconds later, the water stopped running and he slid open the door. And froze.

She smiled at him, forcing herself not to back down now. "Hello," she said softly.

"Hello," he mumbled, his hand reaching for a towel.

"You aren't embarrassed?" she asked, staring blatantly at him, her eyes brimming over with appreciation for the sheer muscular power of his tall, hard body.

He considered that for a minute, and his green eyes glittered as they ran over her. "No, not really," he said. "Not with you."

He was thinking about the scars, she knew, one of the tiny insecurities that underlay all that magnificent pride and arrogance. She got up gracefully from the stool and moved to stand in front of him. Her hand took the towel from his.

"Jude . . ." Her nerve was beginning to fail.

He drew her hands to his body and draped the

towel over them. "You've come this far," he whispered. "Don't get cold feet now."

Her lips parted on a shaky rush of breath as she studied his hard, dark face. "I want to make love to you tonight," she whispered. "You said once that when I was ready, I should come and get you."

A corner of his mouth curved, although his chest was rising and falling in shudders. "Is this a seduction?"

"Well, sort of," she admitted, peeking up at him. "You'll have to guide me. I don't really make a habit of this, like some people I could name."

"You're wasting time," he murmured, glancing down. "And we're running out of it."

Her eyes followed his and jerked back up again.

He laughed softly at her flush. "This was your idea. Take off that robe."

"But I haven't dried you off yet," she whispered.

"I've always had this wild fantasy of being toweled dry by a nude pregnant woman," he murmured drily. "Take it off. If I'm not embarrassed, with my flaws, why in hell should you be?"

She reached up and pressed her fingers to his lips. "You aren't flawed," she said quietly. "I love all of you, every inch, and those scars are marks of courage." She dropped her eyes to his mouth and managed to smile. "When I know you better, I'll kiss every one of them."

He laughed delightedly. "When you know me better?"

"Well, we've only slept together twice," she reminded him. "We're practically strangers."

"We'll get acquainted a lot quicker if you'll take off that damned robe."

She sighed. "You'll never get dried off if I do."

"Think so?"

Her hands went to the belt and she untied the robe, watching his face, and let it fall. His breath caught and his eyes went dark. His chest began to heave.

Her hands slid from his waist up to his head and, trembling, they began to make a small effort to dry his thick hair. But meanwhile, her body had touched his, and he cried out.

"Jude!" she whispered, shaken.

His hands drew her against him. He enfolded her, his arms cradled her, his mouth searched urgently for hers.

"I need you," he whispered unsteadily. "I want you, so much!"

Her lips nibbled at his, teasing, playing, until his hand caught in her long hair and pulled, making her mouth open suddenly as his took it. He rocked her against the hardness of his virile body, and she went weak-kneed with hunger for him.

"I can't wait," he bit off, lifting her. "I'm sorry, honey, I can't wait another second!"

"It's all right," she whispered back, arching her back as his lips found her breasts and worshipped their curves, slid down to the slight rise of her belly.

He laid her down on the bed and her arms pulled him over her.

"The baby," he whispered protectively, hesitating.

"Just don't be too rough, darling," she whispered. Her fingers touched his chest, his waistline, his hips. She found his hands and moved them to her own hips. "Hold me like this," she breathed, "the way you did in the woods that day. . . ."

"Bess!" he groaned, and found her lips with his.

"I love you," she whispered into his seeking mouth. "I love you."

"Do you know what you're saying?" he whispered back, shifting his body so that they moved quickly into a devastating intimacy.

"Yes, I know." She lifted, arched, opening her eyes. "Love me back, just a little, darling," she whispered. "Just a little, even if this is all . . . all you can give . . . Jude!" She gasped, twisting helplessly as his body began the deep, soft motion she remembered, as his tender hands touched her in more intimate ways.

"It's going to be love this time," he said huskily. "On both sides. For both of us, Bess. You're my life, my heart, my world!"

Warmth flooded her body like fire as the words penetrated, and she saw the truth of them in the loving eyes that looked down into hers. "Darling . . . !" she cried out, clinging.

His hands went under her. "Move with me," he breathed, bending to her mouth. "Yes, hard, like that . . . Bess, oh God, Bess, Bess, I love you, I love you . . . !"

He whispered the words like a litany, until they became a breathless, hoarse chant, until her own voice caught and echoed them, until her body and her soul fused with his in one, explosive burst of color that shattered before her startled eyes like a kaleidoscope of shimmering rainbows.

She was hardly aware of time after that. It seemed that they'd only just finished when the symphony of movement and passion began all over again, with tender, soft kisses growing deeper and bodies kindling each other with brushing, teasing contact. He drew her back into his arms, and then every touch seemed to be more intimate, every kiss longer and deeper, every gasp and sob and moan louder than the one before. And this time he taught her things that made him cry out, ways of touching and tasting that gave her power over him, and she gloried in the pleasure she could see him experiencing. Until he reached a point on the edge of his control and, with a harsh groan, moved over her trembling body and, shivering with frank desire, gave her the satisfaction she pleaded for. Finally, from sheer exhaustion, they pulled up the covers and pressed themselves into each other's arms. And slept until morning.

He woke, and woke her, and as the sun filtered in through the blinds, they made love to the sound of birds rousing in the trees outside the window. And it was just as sweet as the night before. They were filled with shared love, with the wonder of belonging to each other.

"And I thought I liked being a bachelor," he murmured drily, ruffling her hair as she lay damply against his hairy chest in the drowsy aftermath of their loving.

She kissed his skin softly. "I'm going to make sure you like being married from now on."

He caressed her face, turning so that he could see her eyes. "Last night was the first time since Christmas," he observed quietly, "that you've reached out for me. Up until then, I'd done it all. All the chasing. All the taking. I used to hope against hope that one night you'd be starving for me and run the truck through my bedroom door," he added on a dry laugh.

"I kind of hoped the same thing," she confessed. "But I wasn't sure of you. I knew you didn't want to get married. I thought if I let you see how much I cared you'd use it against me. And, too, I was furious about Crystal."

He kissed her forehead gently. "Bess, I did hate the idea of marriage when you first came here. But after the first few weeks, it got to the point that I couldn't think of anything but you." He smiled. "I put up trees I didn't want, I went to unbelievable lengths to get my hands on a painting you'd said you liked, I let you set limits for Katy and watched you get her interested in dresses and parties—all the things I swore I wouldn't do. I saw you with her, how you laughed and played. And I wanted to play, too, but it had been too long, and I didn't know how anymore."

She bit gently at his shoulder. "Katy and I can teach you."

"I tried so hard to make you care," he said, and it all showed in his face, all the pain and hunger and frustration that he'd kept her from seeing. "But I couldn't get near you. And that night when you said you didn't want me . . ."

She touched his mouth. "I wanted you very much, I always have. I wanted you when I was fifteen years old, Jude," she confessed fervently. "I don't even know when it became love. But I know one thing. I couldn't survive away from you."

He traced her lips with a long finger. "That goes double for me, Mrs. Langston. I don't much like sleeping alone, either. Do you suppose you might sleep with me from now on?"

"We'd like that," she said.

"We?" He lifted an eyebrow.

She snuggled close with a smile. "Your son and I. Katy's ecstatic, did you notice?"

"Yes, and I'm glad." He drew her closer.

She looked up. "Don't you think I'm sexy?"

"God, yes!" he laughed. "I'll still love you when you look like a pumpkin. I just hope my arms are going to be long enough to reach around you."

She laughed delightedly. "What stories we'll be able to tell our grandchildren," she murmured. "I can just see their faces when I tell them about how you carried me bodily out of Oakgrove and flew me to Texas to get married."

"If you do," he warned, "I'll tell them how you seduced me on the bridle path."

"Blackmailer."

He grinned, rubbing his nose against hers. "We'll keep our secrets, then. Just for the two of us. And when I'm old, I'll whisper memories into your ear in front of them and watch you blush. And I'll be young, and so will you, all over again."

She brushed her fingers over his stubbled cheek lovingly, searching his eyes. "I'll love you all my life."

He kissed her softly. "I'll love you all of mine. Every minute." He sat up, stretching. "How about breakfast? Then we could go into San Antonio and have lunch at that restaurant on the river walk."

"Only if you promise not to stand up and start insulting me."

"Would I do that to a pregnant lady?" he asked. His eyes wandered slowly over her as he got to his feet and he smiled slowly, seductively. "You're pretty like that, in bed. I could lose my head over you."

She lay back on the pillows with a soft sigh, and moved her legs. "Could you? How exciting. Lie down and let's discuss it."

"You witch," he murmured.

She held out her arms. "It's so lonely here in this enormous bed."

"I've got phone calls to make . . ."

Her back arched softly. "I have this terrible ache, darling . . ."

He threw himself down beside her. "To hell with the phone calls. I've got an ache of my own."

Her lips parted and his moved onto them. She

smiled, feeling as if there were champagne in her veins, bubbling and bursting with life and joy and delicious flavor. Her hands ran over the smooth, powerful muscles of his back with sweet abandon. Somehow, he didn't feel at all like rawhide anymore.

YOU'LL BE SWEPT AWAY WITH SILHOUETTE DESIRE

$1.75 each

1 ☐ James
2 ☐ Monet
3 ☐ Clay
4 ☐ Carey

5 ☐ Baker
6 ☐ Mallory
7 ☐ St. Claire

8 ☐ Dee
9 ☐ Simms
10 ☐ Smith

$1.95 each

11 ☐ James
12 ☐ Palmer
13 ☐ Wallace
14 ☐ Valley
15 ☐ Vernon
16 ☐ Major
17 ☐ Simms
18 ☐ Ross
19 ☐ James
20 ☐ Allison
21 ☐ Baker
22 ☐ Durant
23 ☐ Sunshine
24 ☐ Baxter
25 ☐ James
26 ☐ Palmer
27 ☐ Conrad
28 ☐ Lovan
29 ☐ Michelle

30 ☐ Lind
31 ☐ James
32 ☐ Clay
33 ☐ Powers
34 ☐ Milan
35 ☐ Major
36 ☐ Summers
37 ☐ James
38 ☐ Douglass
39 ☐ Monet
40 ☐ Mallory
41 ☐ St. Claire
42 ☐ Stewart
43 ☐ Simms
44 ☐ West
45 ☐ Clay
46 ☐ Chance
47 ☐ Michelle
48 ☐ Powers

49 ☐ James
50 ☐ Palmer
51 ☐ Lind
52 ☐ Morgan
53 ☐ Joyce
54 ☐ Fulford
55 ☐ James
56 ☐ Douglass
57 ☐ Michelle
58 ☐ Mallory
59 ☐ Powers
60 ☐ Dennis
61 ☐ Simms
62 ☐ Monet
63 ☐ Dee
64 ☐ Milan
65 ☐ Allison
66 ☐ Langtry
67 ☐ James

68 ☐ Browning
69 ☐ Carey
70 ☐ Victor
71 ☐ Joyce
72 ☐ Hart
73 ☐ St. Clair
74 ☐ Douglass
75 ☐ McKenna
76 ☐ Michelle
77 ☐ Lowell
78 ☐ Barber
79 ☐ Simms
80 ☐ Palmer
81 ☐ Kennedy
82 ☐ Clay
83 ☐ Chance
84 ☐ Powers
85 ☐ James
86 ☐ Malek

Silhouette Desire

$1.95 each

87 ☐ Michelle	106 ☐ Michelle	125 ☐ Cairni	144 ☐ Evans
88 ☐ Trevor	107 ☐ Chance	126 ☐ Carey	145 ☐ James
89 ☐ Ross	108 ☐ Gladstone	127 ☐ James	146 ☐ Knight
90 ☐ Roszel	109 ☐ Simms	128 ☐ Michelle	147 ☐ Scott
91 ☐ Browning	110 ☐ Palmer	129 ☐ Bishop	148 ☐ Powers
92 ☐ Carey	111 ☐ Browning	130 ☐ Blair	149 ☐ Galt
93 ☐ Berk	112 ☐ Nicole	131 ☐ Larson	150 ☐ Simms
94 ☐ Robbins	113 ☐ Cresswell	132 ☐ McCoy	151 ☐ Major
95 ☐ Summers	114 ☐ Ross	133 ☐ Monet	152 ☐ Michelle
96 ☐ Milan	115 ☐ James	134 ☐ McKenna	153 ☐ Milan
97 ☐ James	116 ☐ Joyce	135 ☐ Charlton	154 ☐ Berk
98 ☐ Joyce	117 ☐ Powers	136 ☐ Martel	155 ☐ Ross
99 ☐ Major	118 ☐ Milan	137 ☐ Ross	156 ☐ Corbett
100 ☐ Howard	119 ☐ John	138 ☐ Chase	157 ☐ Palmer
101 ☐ Morgan	120 ☐ Clay	139 ☐ St. Claire	158 ☐ Cameron
102 ☐ Palmer	121 ☐ Browning	140 ☐ Joyce	159 ☐ St. George
103 ☐ James	122 ☐ Trent	141 ☐ Morgan	160 ☐ McIntyre
104 ☐ Chase	123 ☐ Paige	142 ☐ Nicole	161 ☐ Nicole
105 ☐ Blair	124 ☐ St. George	143 ☐ Allison	162 ☐ Horton

SILHOUETTE DESIRE, Department SD/6
1230 Avenue of the Americas
New York, NY 10020

Please send me the books I have checked above. I am enclosing $_____
(please add 75¢ to cover postage and handling. NYS and NYC residents please
add appropriate sales tax). Send check or money order—no cash or C.O.D.'s
please. Allow six weeks for delivery.

NAME_____

ADDRESS_____

CITY_____STATE/ZIP_____

For the woman who expects a little more out of love, get Silhouette Special Edition.

Take 4 books free — no strings attached.

If you yearn to experience more passion and pleasure in your romance reading ... to share even the most private moments of romance and sensual love between spirited heroines and their ardent lovers, then Silhouette Special Edition has everything you've been looking for.

Get 6 books each month before they are available anywhere else!

Act now and we'll send you four exciting Silhouette Special Edition romance novels. They're our gift to introduce you to our convenient home subscription service. Every month, we'll send you six new passion-filled Special Edition books. Look them over for 15 days. If you keep them, pay just $11.70 for all six. Or return them at no charge.

We'll mail your books to you *two full months before they are available* anywhere else. Plus, with every shipment, you'll receive the Silhouette Books Newsletter absolutely free. *And with Silhouette Special Edition there are never any shipping or handling charges.*

Mail the coupon today to get your four free books — and more romance than you ever bargained for.

Silhouette Special Edition is a service mark and a registered trademark of Simon & Schuster, Inc.